Way Down Deep

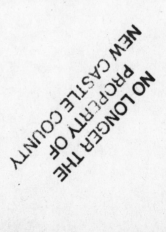

ALSO by RUTH WHITE

The Search for Belle Prater
Buttermilk Hill
Tadpole
Memories of Summer
Belle Prater's Boy
Weeping Willow
Sweet Creek Holler

Way Down Deep

Ruth White

SQUARE
FISH

FARRAR STRAUS GIROUX
NEW YORK

SQUARE
FISH

An Imprint of Macmillan

WAY DOWN DEEP. Copyright © 2007 by Ruth White.
Map copyright © 2007 by Susy Pilgrim Waters for Lilla Rogers Studio.
All rights reserved. Printed in September 2011 in the United States of America
by R. R. Donnelley & Sons Company, Harrisonburg, Virginia. For information,
address Square Fish, 175 Fifth Avenue, New York, NY 10010.

Square Fish and the Square Fish logo are trademarks of Macmillan and are used
by Farrar Straus Giroux under license from Macmillan.

Library of Congress Cataloging-in-Publication Data
White, Ruth, date.
    Way Down Deep / Ruth White.
        p.   cm.
    Summary: In the West Virginia town of Way Down Deep in the 1950s, a
foundling called Ruby June is happily living with Miss Arbutus at the local
boardinghouse when suddenly, after the arrival of a family of outsiders, the
mystery of Ruby's past begins to unravel.
    ISBN 978-0-312-66096-3
    [1. Foundlings—Fiction. 2. Community Life—Fiction. 3. Identity—
Fiction. 4. Orphans—Fiction. 5. West Virginia—History—1951–
—Fiction.] I. Title.

PZ7.W58446 Way 2007
[Fic]—dc22

                                                              2006046324

Originally published in the United States by Farrar Straus Giroux
First Square Fish Edition: October 2011
Square Fish logo designed by Filomena Tuosto
Book designed by Barbara Grzeslo
mackids.com

10 9 8 7 6 5 4 3 2 1

AR: 4.8 / F&P: U

Dedicated to Dee & Dory, William & Wally

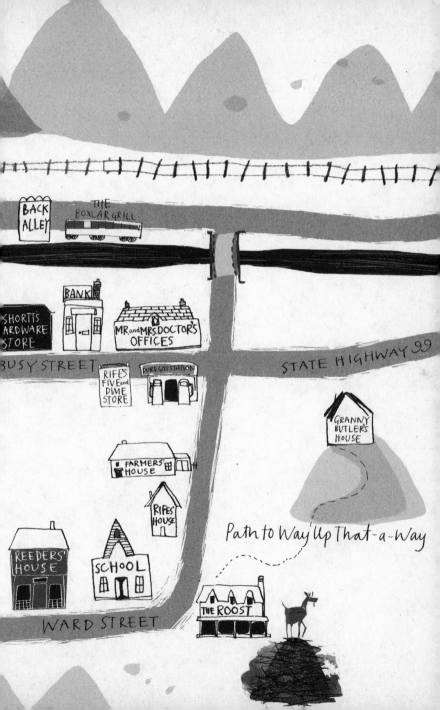

CAST
of
CHARACTERS

ARISTOTLE: a very old and very wise owl

BEVINS, MR.: the town barber and owner of Bevins's
Barber Shop

BEVINS, MRS.: Mr. Bevins's wife, a very fashionable
dresser

BEVINS, LANTHA: the Bevinses' teenage daughter

BUTLER, GRANNY: an old albino woman who keeps bees
Way Up That-a-Way

CHAMBERS, MR.: mayor of Way Down Deep and owner of
the A&P Grocery Store

CHAMBERS, WALLY: son of the mayor

CHAMBERS, SHELBY: the bank teller, and wife of Wally

COMBS, GOLDIE: an old woman who lives on Yonder
Mountain

COMBS, CHRISTIAN: Goldie's son

COMBS, MAXINE: Christian's wife

COMBS, JEFF, SAM, AND SIDNEY: Christian's sons

CRAWFORD, A. H.: a boarder at The Roost, who is writing
a book about the town

DALES, MR.: president of Way Down Bank

DEEL, ELBERT: a circuit-riding judge

ELKINS, MRS. THORNTON: a permanent resident at The
    Roost

FARMER, MR.: the town drunk

FARMER, MRS.: his wife, the postmistress

FULLER, CONNIE LYNN, SUNNY GAYE, AND BONNIE CLARE:
    the Fuller triplets, who preach the Gospel in the
    streets

GENTRY, MR.: a boarder at the Roost, the high school
    band director

HOLLAND, MR.: a detective from Virginia

HORTON, LESTER: a traveler with a baby goat

HURLEY, JOLENE COMBS: Goldie Combs's deceased
    daughter

HURLEY, CLAYTON: husband to Jolene

JETHRO: Ruby's pet goat

JUNE, RUBY: redheaded toddler abandoned in Way Down

JUSTUS, DR.: the town physician, called Mr. Doctor

JUSTUS, DR.: the town dentist, called Mrs. Doctor

MORGAN, MR. AND MRS.: owners of Morgan's Drugs

MORGAN, JUANITA, JUDE, EDNA, AND SLIM: the Morgan
    children

MULLINS, MR. & MRS.: owners of the Pure Gas Station
    and The Boxcar Grill

MULLINS, REESE, MARY NELL, SUSIE, PAULINE, JUNIOR,
    CLARENCE, AND GERRY JOY: the Mullins children, who
    help their parents at the gas station and the grill

REEDER, BOB: Robber Bob, a would-be bank robber

REEDER, BIRD: Robber Bob's senile father

REEDER, PETER, CEDAR, JEETER, SKEETER, AND RITA: the
Reeder kids

REYNOLDS, SHERIFF: sheriff of Way Down

RIFE, MRS.: the ninety-year-old owner of Rife's Five and
Dime

RIFE, WALTER: son of Mrs. Rife; runs the five-and-dime
store

RIPPLE: a red fox

SHORTT, MRS.: the owner of Shortt's Hardware Store

STACEY, MR.: the milkman

WARD, ARCHIBALD: the founder of the town of Way Down
Deep

WARD, MISS ARBUTUS: a direct descendant of Archibald,
and proprietor of a boardinghouse called The Roost

WORLY, MISS: a boarder at the Roost, and the town
librarian

1

To understand the name WAY DOWN DEEP, one must go back to the eighteenth century and the days of adventurers and pioneers. For it was then that an Englishman by the name of Archibald Ward, while exploring the wild Appalachians, stumbled upon a deep hollow cradled between the hills in a place that later became known as West Virginia.

"This is perfect," Archibald said to himself. "I shall bring my loved ones here and start a settlement."

When he returned to civilization back east for the purpose of retrieving his family, people questioned Archibald about his findings, with the idea of perhaps following him to this wilderness.

"What kind of place is it?" they asked him.

"The timber is pale, the sod black, and a stream runs through it," Archibald told them. "And it is naturally sheltered like a nest way down deep in a narrow valley."

People did follow Archibald Ward and started a town in the way-down-deep hollow between the hills. The name caught on, but over the years was often shortened to Way Down. The stream became Way Down Deep Creek, but that being too much of a mouthful, was abridged to Deep Creek. Strictly speaking, however, the stream was not deep, nor was it a creek. It was a puny river.

In the 1840s the fourth Archibald Ward built a boardinghouse in Way Down, which he called The Roost. It remained in the same family one hundred years later, when Miss Arbutus Ward took possession of it at the death of her father. She was an only child and the last Ward left in town. Miss Arbutus had been helping out at The Roost since she was barely big enough to peep over the rim of the giant oak eating table. She knew no other life.

Miss Arbutus was—sad to say—plain and dull. Everybody said so. And there was no telling how old she was— somewhere over thirty. The townsfolk called her an old maid, but they would never use that distasteful term in her presence. She had been outside of Way Down only a few times in her girlhood, and never in her adult life. She preferred The Roost to any other place on earth, and felt most comfortable when she was there.

For a meager amount of money, a weary traveler could eat a wholesome supper at The Roost, sleep between clean sheets, and wake up to a hearty breakfast. The midday meal, which was locally called dinner, was not offered to guests.

Many boarders were total strangers who appeared out of nowhere and went back to nowhere after a day or two, and were never seen again. But some returning guests showed up periodically. The most common were traveling salesmen who came hawking everything from encyclopedias to vacuum cleaners to insurance. The Bible peddler was also a regular. He was a circuit-riding evangelist who, when he got wound up good, preached a right decent sermon to the folks living far back in the hollers. Another regular was Judge Elbert Deel, who was responsible for holding court in three counties.

As for the permanent residents of The Roost, there was an elegant lady who lived on the second floor and insisted on being called by her late husband's whole name.

"Mrs. Thornton Elkins," she would say in her thin, melodious voice. "That's who I am and always will be."

Mr. and Mrs. Thornton Elkins had been married for less than a year when Mr. Elkins was killed in a sawmill accident where he worked near Way Down. Mrs. Thornton Elkins came to The Roost to recuperate for a few weeks, then a few months, then a few years. When she ran out of money, she stayed on. The Wards knew that she had nowhere else to go. So what was a body to do? You certainly could not turn her out in the street, now could you?

Townspeople who knew Mrs. Thornton Elkins's situation sometimes dropped off bolts of dress material for her at The Roost, which she accepted without comment. She borrowed Miss Arbutus's sewing machine to make simple but stylish dresses for herself. Others donated various items known to be necessary to a refined lady of the day, and she got by.

There were less generous souls who were of the opinion that perhaps Mrs. Thornton Elkins should earn her keep by assisting Miss Arbutus in the kitchen, or in the laundry room, or in the garden. But they were not bold enough to broach the subject to that cultured lady, and such an idea would never enter Mrs. Thornton Elkins's head on its own, nor Miss Arbutus's either, for that matter.

There were three other tenants who made The Roost their home. One was Miss Worly, the town librarian. She also lived on the second floor, next to Mrs. Thornton Elkins. Miss Worly referred to her room as her "spacious pastel boudoir."

Because Miss Worly delighted in peppering her sentences with fancy words like *whereby*, *heretofore*, *notwithstanding*, *inasmuch*, *moreover*, and even *albeit* and *i.e.* on occasion, the kids in town called her Miss Wordy, but she didn't mind.

Two middle-aged bachelors occupied the third floor. They were Mr. Gentry, the high school band director, and Mr. Crawford, a somewhat gloomy man of independent means, who had been working for years on a book called *A Colorful History of Way Down Deep, West Virginia*. Nobody had ever seen a page of it, but when the townspeople asked him how the book was progressing, he always replied, "Splendidly! Splendidly!"

The other permanent guests at The Roost knew the truth—that Mr. Crawford had the dreadful habit of wasting perfectly good daylight, sleeping for hours and hours, while his clunky black typewriter collected dust.

2

I N THE EARLY MORNING HOURS OF THE FIRST DAY OF SUM-
mer, 1944, a small redheaded girl was abandoned in
front of Way Down Deep's courthouse. Maybe she was
two and a half, three at the most. Nobody could tell for
sure, and the child could not say.

It was the circuit judge, Elbert Deel, who found her as
he was going to court, after his breakfast at The Roost.

"She was in her petticoat, just sitting there on that
bench where the old-timers like to hang out and swap
lies," Judge Deel often recalled in later years to people
who wanted to hear the story. "She was swinging her bare
feet and babbling to herself."

As the stores began to open, the proprietors spotted
the judge in front of the courthouse talking to a toddler
with a mess of bright curls you couldn't miss from any
point on Busy Street. Naturally, they had to go investigate.

Walter Rife, who ran the five-and-dime store owned
by his mother, came first. He was followed by Mr. and
Mrs. Doctor, the prominent Mr. Dales, Mr. Bevins, Mrs.

Morgan, Mrs. Farmer, Mayor Chambers, Mrs. Shortt, Mr. Mullins, and everybody else all in a bunch.

"What is your name, dear child?" someone said to the girl.

The child pointed to herself, as small ones do, and said, "Me Woo-bee."

"Woo-bee?"

She nodded. "Me Woo-bee."

"Is she saying Ruby?"

"Yes, I think so. Ruby, is that your name, Ruby?"

The child smiled and nodded. "Me Woo-bee."

"Well, Ruby, where is your mommie? Where is your daddy?"

"Dunno."

"What is your daddy's name?"

"Dada."

"What do other people call him?"

Ruby stuck her fingers in her mouth.

"How did you get here, Ruby?"

"Wide."

"Wide? Oh, ride? Ride in a car?"

"Wide hossie."

"Ride what? Oh! A horsie? You came on a horse?"

Ruby nodded her red head vigorously. "Wide hossie."

The people looked at each other with puzzled expressions. They could not think of anybody hereabouts who rode a horse.

Sheriff Reynolds pushed his way to the center of the crowd, and stood looking at the child. He was in his shirtsleeves that day because his only uniform was at the dry cleaner's.

"What is it?" he said, as if he did not recognize Ruby as being a member of his own species.

"Somebody left her here."

"Her name's Ruby."

"Can we keep her?"

Mr. and Mrs. Doctor took Ruby to their offices for observation. Mr. Doctor was the town's only physician, and his wife, Mrs. Doctor, was the dentist. Their surname was Justus, but nobody ever called them by it.

Ruby promptly fell asleep, and Mrs. Doctor put her to bed.

"She must have been up all night," Mrs. Doctor said sympathetically. "Poor baby."

In Way Down, news was quick to make the rounds, and so it was that Miss Arbutus Ward heard about the child from one of her boarders. Though she was known in the town to be somewhat remote, and not fond of talking to people, she wasted no time in walking to the sheriff's office in the heat of the day, and stating her purpose.

"I want the girl, Sheriff," was exactly what Miss Arbutus said. "I'll take good care of her—that is, until you find her people." And she said no more. Just stood there as tall and thin as an evening shadow, waiting for his answer.

Sheriff Reynolds was so taken aback by Miss Arbutus's sudden appearance in his office, he didn't know how to react. For a long moment, he simply sat there gaping at her.

But to tell the truth, he couldn't say no to Miss Arbutus, or to anybody else for that matter. So he finally mumbled, "Okay."

To tell another truth, the sheriff's heart was way too soft and his mind too fuzzy for sheriffing. Why, he had no idea where to begin this investigation. He had no clues to go on, unless you took the horse into account, but nobody believed for a moment that Ruby came into their town on a horse. Just a child's fantasy.

The next day, in the town's only newspaper, *The Way Down Deep Daily*, there was a blurry picture of the little girl sitting on Mr. Doctor's desk, with the caption

DO YOU KNOW THIS CHILD?

The sheriff didn't know what else he should do, so he did nothing, and as the days and weeks went by, he did even less.

Way Down was a town that did not do things by the book. For example, they didn't know the meaning of social services. And that's why Ruby never became a ward of the county or the state, or any person, for that matter. Even Judge Deel looked the other way.

Besides, the good citizens of Way Down reckoned if Ruby's people were dumb enough to lose something as valuable as a child, then finders keepers, losers weepers.

However, they commiserated, Miss Arbutus was alone, bless her heart. She had lost her father, who was the last member of her family, only a few months earlier. So she was welcome to oversee the child's upbringing, if that was what she craved. And, obviously, it was.

Ruby was given a room of her own on the first floor right beside Miss Arbutus's chamber in the ancient rambling three-story boardinghouse. Miss Arbutus had slept in that same room as a child, and her parents had slept in the room which Miss Arbutus presently occupied.

Those first weeks Ruby didn't seem to miss her mommie or daddy or anybody else who might have been a part of her brief history. In fact, her previous life seemed to evaporate from her mind like fog in the morning sun. She settled into life at The Roost, as content as a cherub on a cloud.

A call went out to the community not to forget the tyke, and Miss Arbutus gratefully accepted small donations on Ruby's behalf. Thus the child thrived, and never wanted for anything.

The Way Down Deep School, located across the street from The Roost, educated all grades. When it seemed Ruby was the right age, she was sent there to learn to read and write, at which time it was necessary to give her a surname.

"She came to us in June," Miss Arbutus said. "We will call her Ruby June."

And so it was.

3

On a rainy evening when Ruby was about seven, a weary traveler rapped upon the door of The Roost, which was an unusual event. Most folks just barged right on in. But this man, who introduced himself as Lester Horton, had a reason for not coming in, and he held that reason with a frayed rope attached to a skinny neck. It was a billy goat.

"I have no money in my pockets," Lester Horton admitted to Miss Arbutus. To prove his statement true, he turned both pockets inside out, revealing nothing but lint. "And I am thumbing my way to Kentucky. Would you please take this baby goat here in exchange for food and shelter for the night?"

"You can stay," Miss Arbutus said, "but I'll not take your pet away from you."

"You might as well," the man said sadly, patting the animal's droopy drippy head. "I don't think the poor little thing will make it to Kentucky."

Miss Arbutus thought about that. "Very well," she said after a moment.

Ruby, who was standing behind Miss Arbutus looking at the goat, was tickled pink. She would be the only child in school who had a goat for a pet!

"I'll take him to the backyard," she volunteered.

"Come on in," Miss Arbutus said to Lester Horton. "Supper's on the table."

Lester Horton was so grateful to Miss Arbutus, he wept. He explained the tears by saying that he was going through a personal crisis.

Ruby named the goat Jethro, and under her care he soon found health. She placed an old rug on the back porch, where he curled up exactly like a dog to sleep at night. A half wall protected him from the elements.

During the day, when he was not busy at his job trimming the grass, Jethro romped and played in the enclosed backyard of The Roost. He developed a particular fondness for the woodpile against the fence, which he climbed daily. From the top he watched for Ruby to come home from school. He could also see most of the town, and often stood there to observe, with great interest, the daily goings-on of the townspeople.

One day, when a life insurance salesman from Hartford, Connecticut, parked his car beside the fence where the woodpile was located, Jethro's slow little goat brain fashioned an idea. Why not step off the wood and onto the roof of the car? He did so, and was absolutely delighted with himself, because from this vantage point the view was much better. The regulars at The Roost soon learned not to park their cars in that spot, but they did not warn the strangers. Why spoil Jethro's fun?

In subsequent years, which were kinder to him, Lester Horton often returned to Way Down to spend a night at The Roost—as a paying guest, of course—to see how the goat got on. He was only one among many visitors who sometimes came to The Roost even when they didn't have business in town.

Upon entering the third grade, Ruby was allowed to help Miss Arbutus take care of the boarders when she was not in school. Her first job was setting the giant oak table in the dining hall every breakfast and supper.

When she had conquered setting the table, filling the glasses with tea or lemonade, and drying the dishes, Ruby learned to take a feather duster to the antique furniture in the spacious common room, and in the bedrooms, while the guests were out.

In time Ruby was sweeping the front porch several times a week. It was wide and wrapped around the front and partially down each side of The Roost. White rocking chairs with small tables between them were scattered about. Boardinghouse guests enjoyed sitting out there and watching the world go by.

Almost every morning in warm weather Ruby found treasures on this porch. There were baskets full of ripe red cherries or strawberries, spring lettuce, pickling cucumbers, tomatoes, string beans, lima beans, beets, corn, melons, peaches, or blackberries—gifts from the townspeople.

As she grew older, Ruby learned to help Miss Arbutus put up the most abundant of these foods for cold weather. She loved to have Jethro at her heels in the backyard as she helped sterilize Mason jars and lids in a big pot of water set over a fire. She also loved puttering about the kitchen with Miss Arbutus, preparing the food for canning. Eventually she found herself helping with the actual cooking of meals, and she was proud.

Ruby also learned to care for the flowers that encircled the porch. Her favorites were the pansies. She adored those chubby faces peering up at her, eagerly looking forward to their daily drink of water. She talked to them, told them how beautiful they were, and watched them shamelessly primp and preen in the sunshine.

Ruby enjoyed all the jobs she was asked to do, but when it was learned that she preferred running errands on Busy Street to everything else, Miss Arbutus purchased a red Radio Flyer wagon for Ruby, and sent her out after school and on the weekends to buy this, to buy that.

Gradually Ruby took over all the shopping for the boardinghouse. It saved Miss Arbutus a lot of time and steps.

Ruby became a familiar sight to the citizens of the town as they encountered her pulling her wagon from The Roost on Ward Street to Busy Street, where the stores were located, and which ran parallel to Deep Creek. Outside of town, Busy Street turned into State Highway 99. It was the only road leading into and out of the valley.

"Good morning, Ruby June."

Way Down folks liked the sound of these two names together, and rarely used one without the other.

"Good morning, Mr. Mullins." (Or Mrs. Farmer, or whoever.)

"Where you going to, Ruby June?"

"To Shortt's Hardware for a new mop bucket."

"Give my regards to Mrs. Shortt, Ruby June."

"Will do, and give my regards to Mrs. Mullins and Reese and Mary Nell and Susie and Pauline and Junior and Clarence and . . . who did I leave out?"

"Gerry Joy."

"Right! Gerry Joy."

"You betcha."

Mr. Mullins owned not only the Pure Gas Station but also a snack bar called The Boxcar Grill. It was actually housed in an abandoned boxcar, with sliding doors and all, on Railroad Street, which ran parallel to the tracks on the other side of Deep Creek. Mrs. Mullins was the short-order cook on that side of the river, while Mr. Mullins pumped gas on this side. They were assisted by the seven children Ruby had sent regards to, who ranged in age from nine to nineteen.

Miss Arbutus had charge accounts at Shortt's Hardware Store, Mayor Chambers's A&P Grocery Store, Morgan's Drugs, and Rife's Five and Dime. All these merchants rewarded their customers with S&H Green Stamps, and Ruby was allowed to keep the stamps for herself. When her errands were finished, she would paste them into her S&H Green Stamp book, and dream of the gifts she planned to redeem them for.

4

By the time Ruby was nine or ten, she and Miss Arbutus had established several pleasant rituals in their daily life. For example, when they were finished with all the boardinghouse business in the evening, they took turns at soaking away the day's accumulation of dirt in an ancient claw-footed tub in their private bathroom, which was tucked between their two rooms.

Afterward they dutifully brushed their teeth up and down with Ipana, slathered their hands and limbs with Jergens, and saturated their faces with Deep Magic, as instructed in advertisements.

Next they went to Miss Arbutus's dressing table, where they took great pains in manicuring their nails. During this ritual Miss Arbutus might gently remind Ruby, "When you're in the habit of preparing food for others, it is essential to have clean fingernails."

Finally Miss Arbutus would take her long brown hair out of its tight bun so that Ruby could brush it. This was the favorite hour of the day for both of them, for at this time, dressed in their long white nightgowns, they shared their day-to-day joys and concerns. Although Miss Arbutus was stingy with words to most people, she was more than generous with Ruby. The subject might be school, or the boarders, or the townspeople, or any old thing that crossed their minds.

"It's rumored that the first Archibald Ward, who was the founder of this town, brought a treasure to Way Down those many years ago," Miss Arbutus said one night.

"Was he a rich man?"

"No, he was not. But he was a very adventurous man, and a traveler. They say he found a pirate's treasure during one of his explorations on the coast of Virginia."

Ruby's eyes grew large. "A pirate's treasure?"

"Yes, gold doubloons and pieces of eight!" Miss Arbutus spoke in a whispery mysterious voice. "And he never used the money because he was afraid the pirates would find him and kill him. So he buried it way down deep somewhere in Way Down Deep, far from the coast and the prying eyes of the world."

"Do you think it's true, Miss Arbutus? Is there really a treasure buried in Way Down?"

"It's a legend, Ruby. All the people who have ever lived here know the story, and have repeated it to their children, so that the truth has probably been distorted. But you know what they say about legends. They are rooted in fact somewhere down the line."

Occasionally, during their evening chats, Miss Arbutus talked about what she had dreamed the previous night. Her dreams were lucid and lively.

"Last night I went to England. I saw Big Ben and Buckingham Palace, where the young princesses reside. I saw Stonehenge and the wild moors where the night wind goes moaning through the gorse, just like Mr. Thomas Hardy said in his books. I saw the White Cliffs of Dover, which our servicemen loved so much during the war. There was a song about it. I saw it all, and talked to the people. I love the way they talk."

"I should like to go to England," Ruby said.

"Well, if we ever find old Archibald Ward's treasure, we will go to England, and all over Europe."

They smiled at each other in the looking glass.

"But we will come home, won't we?" Ruby said. "We'll always come back to Way Down?"

"Of course we will. I got homesick even in my dream. So I turned my face toward America, and crossed the briny Atlantic Ocean with my bare feet running like a riverboat paddle across the waves. Sometimes I scampered across the backs of whales. A school of dolphins tried to keep up with me, but they could not. I saw them leaping in the moonlight. When I woke up, the bottom ruffle of my nightgown was wet, and little bitty strings of seaweed were clinging to it."

Once Ruby asked Miss Arbutus, "Did you have such vivid dreams when you were small like me?"

And Miss Arbutus responded, "Oh, yes. When I was

about ten I had a dog called Stinky. I named him that because he loved to roll in smelly stuff, and he got a bath more often than I did. Anyway, when he was clean, he slept at the foot of my bed.

"One night when I was suffering from a high fever, I had a nightmare. I dreamed that Stinky and I were climbing around the edge of a volcano when I suddenly slipped and fell. I fell and fell for the longest time, and I knew that I would land in a pool of fiery lava! I could feel the heat rising to meet me. Then I heard Stinky. I looked up and saw him peeping down at me over the rim of the volcano, and barking his silly head off. He was urging me to wake up! Wake up! Wake up!

"And I actually did come to myself in my own bed, drenched with sweat. My fever had broken. Stinky was there sleeping at my feet, twitching and whimpering. I knew he was still in the dream, so I shook him awake. He was so tickled to see me alive, he jumped all over me and licked my face."

When they grew weary, Ruby would go to her cozy room, which Miss Arbutus had decorated for her in ruffled yellow and white, with purple pansies embroidered on her curtains and pillow shams.

Before turning out the light, Ruby always stood before the window and gazed at the hills against the night sky. Though she could not remember her parents, she thought of them, and wished them health and happiness.

"And don't forget me," she always added. "Woo-bee is right here waiting for you."

Then Ruby climbed into bed. The pansy curtains fluttered in the mountain breeze as her eyes closed. Sometimes she woke up in the wee hours of the morning to find a lady in her room, sitting very still in an armchair by the window. At such times a hazy memory floated to the surface of Ruby's mind—a memory of being held and rocked beside a window, through which she could see snow falling.

If Ruby sat up in bed, or said anything, the woman disappeared into the shadows. So she learned that if she was to keep this lady, who was *surely* her mother, then she must not move or speak. She would drift off to sleep again, and the morning daylight revealed nobody in the chair.

5

IN HER SUMMER SHORTS AND SANDALS, RUBY WAS PULLING the Radio Flyer down Ward Street on her way to the bank on a bright Monday before noon. Having passed the seventh grade, she was soon to celebrate another birthday—which was believed to be her thirteenth—on the anniversary of her sudden appearance at the courthouse.

School had closed on Friday, and to the children of Way Down it was the beginning of summer, even though that season had not officially arrived by the calendar.

Ruby was deep in daydreams about what she would buy on her birthday with her current batch of S&H Green Stamps, when suddenly she heard somebody shrieking.

"Take that, you little monster!"

"Ouch!" Someone else yelped in pain.

Ruby stopped walking. Ahead she could see Reese Mullins from The Boxcar Grill. He was in Ruby's grade at school.

"Not again!" Ruby said out loud, for she knew what

the yelling was all about. Ninety-year-old Mrs. Rife, owner of Rife's Five and Dime Store, was throwing rocks. She had been doing this off and on ever since she retired from the store about five years before.

On several occasions, Mayor Chambers had scolded Mrs. Rife about that very bad habit of hers, but she would pretend she couldn't hear him.

"Say what? Say what?" she would screech at him, holding a hand up to her ear. "You'll have to speak louder. I'm old and nearly deef!"

The mayor had been heard to comment that while some old people were hard of hearing, Mrs. Rife was simply hard of listening.

What Ruby usually did during these rock-throwing episodes was try to hide behind other people's shrubs as she approached Mrs. Rife's house—not an easy task when you're pulling a wagon. Upon reaching the Rife house, she would make a mad dash down the sidewalk.

It wasn't too hard to get out of Mrs. Rife's range. For one thing, she stood on her front porch, which was a good piece from the street, and for another, she couldn't throw hard. Furthermore, the rocks Mrs. Rife selected were not large, but they still hurt, and the old lady's age didn't seem to interfere with her aim.

Ruby sprinted just in time. A rock whizzed by her head.

"I'll get you yet!" Mrs. Rife hollered. "You mangy stray!"

Ruby caught up with Reese, who was holding his elbow. Well, at least he hadn't been hit in the head.

"You okay, Reese?"

"Yeah," he said, glancing back at Mrs. Rife with a scowl. "What's the matter with that nutty old woman?"

"You said it—she's nutty," Ruby said. "Where you going to?"

"I'm going back to work. I took some sandwiches to the crew that's fixing up the schoolhouse. They tipped me, see?"

He showed a nickel in the palm of his hand. "Can I buy you a Hershey bar with my nickel, Ruby June?"

All the townspeople considered Ruby a natural beauty, but to Reese she was the girl of his dreams. He had never hidden the fact that he liked her better than anybody.

Ruby shook her head. "No thanks, Reese. You keep your nickel."

"Will you come and eat dinner with me at The Boxcar?"

"I can't, Reese, but I thank you kindly."

"I'll fix you a hot dog with chili and a bottle of pop, no charge."

"That would be real good, Reese, but I can't make it today."

"Another day?"

"Maybe."

"Tomorrow?"

"No."

They were approaching Busy Street, where Ruby would turn to go to the bank and Reese would keep going straight to cross the bridge over Deep Creek to The Boxcar Grill.

"This nickel reminds me of a song. Can I sing it to you, Ruby June?"

He was always being reminded of some silly song or other.

"No! Bye, Reese." And she began to run—fast.

Reese started singing anyhow. She knew he would. In his own mind he was the second coming of Hank Williams, but to everybody else he was as off-key as a hillbilly slung up drunk on moonshine. And was he *loud*!

"Now if I had a nickel I know what I would do
I'd spend it all for candy and give it all to you . . .
'Cause that's how much I love you, baby!
That's how much I love you!"

The people on the street were much amused at the spectacle of Reese Mullins trying to sing a love song to Ruby June.

"Ain't that the cutest thing?" they said to one another as they stopped to watch.

"Look at Ruby June's face, would you? It's as red as her hair!"

Ruby's empty wagon clanged along behind her, so

noisy it nearabout drowned out Reese's song—nearabout, but not quite.

> *"Now if you were a horsefly and I an old grey mare,*
> *I'd stand and let you bite me and never move a hair . . .*
> *'Cause that's how much I love you, baby!*
> *That's how much I love you!"*

Ruby rushed past the offices of Mr. and Mrs. Doctor, parked her wagon outside the bank, and hurried inside, relieved to close the door behind her.

6

RUBY WELCOMED THE PEACE AND COOLNESS INSIDE THE
bank. It was all dark wood and wine carpet, and had
the only chandelier in town. It dangled over the heads of
several customers waiting in line. One of them was a
stranger—an unusually short man wearing denim overalls
and a T-shirt.

The lone teller finished with one customer, another
approached the window, and the stranger moved to the
head of the line as Ruby took her place at the end. Mrs.
Bevins, the barber's wife, was in front of her. This lady
was much celebrated in Way Down for her extraordinary
wardrobe. She often went to Charleston to shop for
clothes.

No other woman in West Virginia would be caught
dead wearing eye shadow in the daytime. But Mrs. Bevins
always painted her eyes to match her outfit. That day
she was wearing a dress of shimmery twill, as green as
a pickle. On her massive feet were dyed-to-match In-
dian moccasins. Ruby wondered if the dye bled on

Mrs. Bevins's feet and made them as green as the rest of her.

There was a reason for Ruby's special attention to the shoes—moccasins were "in." She thought Miss Arbutus might give her a pair for her birthday, white ones, of course.

"Good morning, Ruby June." Mrs. Bevins turned to speak to her.

"Good morning, Mrs. Bevins. I love your outfit."

"Thank you, Ruby June." Mrs. Bevins flushed, fluttered her eyelids, and gave the green dress a slight swirl. "Just something I threw together."

"And how's the family, Mrs. Bevins?"

"Doing good, except for Lantha. She's a bit peaked with a summer cold."

"Ooo, poor thing," Ruby sympathized. "I always say there's nothing nastier than a summer cold. Why, you don't mind a cold in January. You expect it, don't you? But who wants a cold when you can't lay out of school?"

Mrs. Morgan, from Morgan's Drug Store, entered the bank and took her place in line behind Ruby.

"Good morning, Ruby June," said Mrs. Morgan.

"Good morning, Mrs. Morgan," she said. "How's Juanita and Jude and Edna and Slim, and Mr. Morgan?"

"In good health, Ruby June, and what are you up to today?"

Ruby produced an envelope from her shorts pocket. "I came in to make a deposit for Miss Arbutus—twenty-five dollars."

"How is Miss Arbutus? I don't reckon I've seen her in a month of Sundays. Is she as backward as ever?"

Ruby did not get a chance to respond, because at that moment the short stranger jumped out of line and started waving a gun around with one hand and a brown paper bag with the other.

"This is a holdup!" he shouted.

The bank customers sucked in air together as if they were fixing to sing on cue.

"Heah me?" the stranger hollered more forcefully. "A holdup! Just do as I say and you won't get hurt."

Except for Mrs. Morgan placing a hand on Ruby's arm, nobody moved. They just stood looking at the man.

"All right, then," the gunman said, handing the bag to the teller. "Here, miss, take this poke and fill it full of money."

"Miss" was Shelby Chambers, a pretty young thing only recently married to Wally Chambers, son of the mayor. She did not take the bag. With one hand on her heart she swayed precariously, the blood drained from her face, and she crumbled like a rag doll onto the floor behind the counter.

"Now what? Now what?" the man muttered, seeming totally confounded.

Mr. Dales, the bank president, appeared from a back office behind the teller's window. He stopped in his tracks and surveyed the scene.

"Fill this poke full of money!" the bank robber shouted at Mr. Dales. "Understand?"

Mr. Dales moved forward, carefully stepped over Shelby, and took the bag from the stranger through the teller's window.

"Just small bills!" the man said sternly.

Calmly, Mr. Dales began filling the bag from a cash drawer.

At the sight of a twenty-dollar bill, the man cried out, "I said no big bills!" His voice cracked, and he finished almost in a whisper. "You can't get nobody to break 'em for you."

"You're no bank robber!" Ruby blurted out.

The man whipped his gun around to point it in Ruby's face. A gasp rose up from the group. Unruffled, Ruby stood almost eye to eye with the dangerous criminal.

"He's crying," she said, with hands planted on hips. "Just look at him. See?"

It was true. Big fat tears were rolling down the bandit's cheeks and onto his T-shirt.

"You're no bank robber," Ruby repeated.

The man stood there holding the gun in Ruby's face—and yes, he bawled. Mrs. Morgan walked to him and placed one hand on his bare arm.

"You don't want to do this, do you?" she said.

"Course I do!" he croaked. "I got five young'uns and they need things. I can't do for them worth a flip."

"That must be hard," Mrs. Morgan said as she patted his arm. With the other hand she touched the gun and gently nudged it away from Ruby's face. The man did not protest.

Mr. Dales dropped the bag and walked through a small swinging gate into the lobby. "You wanna give me your weapon, friend?" he said to the man, holding out his hand.

"Weapon?" The man looked at his gun through tears. "You mean this weapon?" he said.

He pointed the gun at Mr. Dales and pulled the trigger.

7

Snap! The gun was plastic.

With this revelation, the bank customers let out a collective breath and gathered round the stranger, their noses fairly twitching with curiosity.

"Charity gave it to my boys for Christmas. I'm scared of real guns," the man said.

At that moment Sheriff Reynolds came in, whistling. Freshly shaved and trimmed at Bevins's Barber Shop, he was looking spiffy in his new blue uniform, which had a gold patch on the sleeve.

The sheriff stopped just inside the door. The cluster of bank customers was like a painting of big-eyed people frozen in place, as they stared at him, but his professionally trained eye was fixed on the stranger with the gun.

"Stop waving that thang around, will you?" the sheriff scolded the short man. "It might go off and hurt somebody!"

The would-be bank robber quickly stashed the toy gun under his overalls bib.

At that moment Shelby came to and pulled herself to her feet. "How much did he get?"

"Hello, Shelby, my girl. What were you doing down there on the floor?" the sheriff said, smiling at her.

She didn't answer.

Not realizing he was breaking in line, because the line was pretty well scattered by then, the sheriff stepped forward and slid a ten-dollar bill through the cubbyhole. "Change that for me, would you, sugar? One one and five fives."

The sheriff glanced around at the other customers, who still did not move, except for Ruby. She was scratching a mosquito bite in that hollow place behind her knee.

"You mean one five and five ones," she corrected the sheriff.

He turned back to Shelby. "What did I say?"

When Shelby didn't answer, Ruby volunteered, "You said one one and five fives."

"Did I?" the sheriff bellowed, and slapped his thigh. "I meant one five and five ones. Bet y'all thought I was trying to pull a fast one, didn't you? Trying to rob the bank or something!" And he laughed so hard, his face turned red and he began to cough.

Shelby, seeing the brown bag half-full of money right there in front of her, retrieved the requested bills from it and passed them to the sheriff, replacing them with his ten-dollar bill.

The sheriff pocketed the money, said thanks, and left, still laughing at his own blunder, and muttering, "One one and five fives. Lordy mercy!"

The door closed behind him.

With the law gone, Mr. Dales placed a hand on the stranger's shoulder and asked, "What's your name, son?"

The man's eyes moved sideways to look at the hand.

"Bob," he squeaked. "Bob Reeder."

"Well, Bob Reeder, I know you did not really mean to rob this bank."

To which Bob Reeder answered in a decidedly biblical manner. "My friends, deep despair has befallen me, and I was sorely tempted into transgression."

He paused and looked around at all the various colors of puzzled eyes watching him. He saw no meanness there, so he continued.

"To put it another way, I am riding high on the crest of a slump."

He paused again and wiped his eyes with his T-shirt sleeve.

"You see, me and my good wife, Pearl, were married for thirteen years, and produced five of the finest offspring who ever breathed. And life was good. But then . . ."

He put his face in his hands. "Well . . . you see," he mumbled through his fingers, "my Pearl left this life six months ago."

His voice quivered. There were sympathetic sounds in the room as many reached out to touch the grieving man.

Bob heaved a weary sigh and sprawled into one of the genuine leatherette chairs Mr. Dales kept there in the lobby.

"That was only the beginning of my troubles," he went on. "Next, my old daddy's brain got so addled, he couldn't tell you the year if he had to. He lives more in the past than the present. Naturally, I took him in so me and the kids could look after him.

"Then my oldest boy, Peter, started catching the tonsilitis every time the weather changed. So his tonsils had to come out, and the doctor bills were awful. Then—"

"Your boy's name is Peter Reeder?" Ruby interrupted him.

Bob nodded and went on. "My second oldest boy, Cedar, started acting like a reg'lar juvenile delinquent, always cussing and acting up soooo bad at school. He makes me ashamed."

"Cedar Reeder?" Ruby mumbled, but Bob Reeder paid her no attention.

"And there's my baby Rita, poor little tyke. She's five, and has not uttered one syllable since her mama died. I just thank the Lord for my nine-year-old twins, Jeeter and Skeeter. They don't give me a lick of trouble.

"If that was not enough," he continued, "I lost my job at the sawmill. Now I can't feed and clothe any of them proper."

"Where might you be from, Mr. Reeder?" Mr. Dales said.

"Y'all call me Bob, heah? I'm from Yonder Mountain. Ever heard of it?"

"Oh, sure, heard of it. Never been there. It's over in Virginia, isn't it?"

"Yeah, just barely."

"How'd you get to Way Down, Bob?"

"On the bus."

"And how were you planning to get away after robbing our bank?"

"On the bus," Bob said.

Bob's listeners were too polite to say what they thought of that dim-witted scheme.

Since serving refreshments to important guests was a custom in the bank, Shelby appeared with a coffeepot and a trayful of cups and cookies. She started to pour coffee for Bob Reeder first, but her hands were trembling so hard, she couldn't hit the cup. Bob Reeder sprang up from his chair and kindly took the pot from her.

"I apologize for giving you the vapors," he said to Shelby. "I hope you will forgive me." And he proceeded to serve the coffee himself.

Shelby smiled a shaky smile and passed around the cookies.

Bob Reeder returned to his seat, took a handful of cookies, and tried to eat them all at once. The others nibbled politely, and looked anywhere except at this unfortunate man in the chair, for he was a pitiful sight.

"I reckon it had been a long time since he saw a cookie," Ruby said that afternoon at Morgan's Drugs, as she and Mrs. Morgan related the story to some of the townspeople who had come in from the heat for an afternoon break.

"Mr. Dales gave him the rest to take home to his kids," Mrs. Morgan added.

Ruby was twirling round and round on one of the soda counter stools. Between sentences, she was biting the caps off of tiny wax Coke bottles and slurping the colored liquid out of them. Walter Rife at Rife's Five and Dime had given them to her, probably trying to make up for the behavior of his mother, the nutty rock thrower.

"The mayor donated a bunch of groceries from his store to the Reeders," Ruby went on.

"And Mr. Dales is arranging for them to come to Way Down and live in his old empty house on Ward Street," Mrs. Morgan added. "Get them close to us, see, so we can all pitch in and help them."

"For inasmuch as ye have done it unto the least of these my brethren, ye have done it unto me!"

The room fell quiet as everybody turned to look at Miss Worly. She and Mr. Gentry were sitting in one of the tall black booths, sipping something cold. The townspeople were surprised to hear Miss Worly quoting Scripture, as she was not known to be religious. No doubt the word *inasmuch*, one of her favorites, had tempted her to do it.

"You said it, Miss Wordy," Ruby said. "The least of these my brethren—that's Robber Bob to a T!"

From that moment to the last day of his life Bob Reeder was known as Robber Bob, and contrary to what one might think, he liked the nickname. He figured anything was better than Shorty.

8

THE TELEPHONE WAS STILL A FAIRLY NEWFANGLED INVEN-
tion to the small towns and hamlets of West Virginia,
and folks were not yet inclined to depend on it for con-
ducting business, which suited Miss Arbutus, for she did
not like to speak into a receiver any more than she liked
talking face-to-face with folks. When she needed to con-
tact somebody outside of town, which was a rare occasion,
she wrote very nice handwritten letters. To Way Down
folks, she sent a messenger.

For the convenience of the boarders, however, there
was indeed a phone at The Roost. The number was
Olive-4000, requested by Miss Arbutus's father because it
would be easy for guests to remember. Rarely did a call
come for reserving a room at The Roost. Most folks just
showed up at the door. But when such a call came, whoever answered the phone took the message for Miss Arbutus.

There were four other residences on the same party

line with The Roost. The phone was located by the fireplace in the common room, and any time you passed through, you were liable to find Mrs. Thornton Elkins curled up there on the sofa, with an ear to the receiver, listening in. She found telephone discussions most interesting and enlightening. So much so, in fact, that sometimes she plumb forgot herself and joined in the conversation.

To be fair, Mrs. Thornton Elkins was not alone in her attraction to the party line. It was common practice for Way Down folks, when they had nothing else to do, to pick up the receiver, and hear what they could hear.

So it was from the party line that the big news spread around town on the following Saturday that Mr. Dales had taken a bunch of boys from town up to Yonder Mountain in his truck that morning to haul the Reeders and their belongings down. They had moved into the green two-story frame house on Ward Street, a few houses beyond The Roost. The Dales family had lived there before they built their new brick ranch out on Highway 99. Mr. Dales was letting the Reeders live there rent-free for the time being.

Ruby refrained from intruding on the newcomers at such a hectic time, but all day her curiosity led her to watch the street for any signs of the new kids. She thought perhaps they would want to look around the neighborhood. It was after supper when she glanced out a front window, and sure enough there was a strange boy and an old man walking on the sidewalk.

"Gonna run down the street for a bit!" she hollered to Miss Arbutus, and hurried out the door.

"Hello!" she called to the strangers. "What's your name?"

The boy turned to her with a shy smile. "I'm Peter Reeder, and this is my granddaddy. Everybody calls him Bird."

"Why do they call him Bird?"

" 'Cause that's his name."

"Oh."

The man jingled when he walked because he had a string of tiny silver bells tied round his ankle.

"How do you do, Bird," Ruby said politely, and held out a hand to the man. "My name is Ruby June."

Bird did not take the hand. Instead he stopped in the middle of the sidewalk and stared at Ruby with a puzzled expression.

"He's not quite all there," Peter apologized as he took his granddaddy's arm.

"Then where's he at?" Ruby asked.

"Floating around somewhere in the past. He's going through his second childhood."

"What are the bells for?" Ruby asked.

"He's liable to wander off and get lost. So the bells let us know where he is."

Peter was about the same age as Ruby, she guessed. He was taller than his daddy, Robber Bob, but he had the same gray eyes. He was tan as a nut and had a mess of blond hair hanging down in his face.

"Where you going to?" Ruby asked him.

"Just to walk around town," he answered. "Maybe I'll see a HELP WANTED sign in a store window."

"Monday morning might be the best time to look for a job," Ruby informed him.

"Well, to be honest, I was thinking Saturday night might be the best time to make friends," Peter said.

"Consider me friend number one, and I'll show you around," Ruby said.

"Sure. I'd like that."

Together they continued toward Busy Street.

"Panthers got 'er," Bird said.

Peter ignored the old man, and said to Ruby, "Do you live in that big white house you came out of?"

Ruby nodded.

"I saw a goat in back of there today. He was standing on the top of a Studebaker."

"That's my Jethro," Ruby replied. "He likes to have a good view of the town."

"You're right handy to the schoolhouse," Peter said. "Just across the road. With the football field over there, I bet you could go up to the top floor of your house and see the games for free, couldn't you?"

"I could, but I just pay my quarter like everybody else."

Peter glanced back over his shoulder at The Roost. "It sure is a nice big house," he said, with admiration in his voice.

"It's a boardinghouse," Ruby explained. "Did you see the sign there over the porch that says 'The Roost'?"

"Yeah, I saw it when we first went by today, but I didn't know what it meant."

"Well, that's what it means. You know, when chickens turn in for the night, people say they are going to roost?"

"Yeah, it's a good name. Does your mama and daddy own The Roost?"

"No, I just live there with Miss Arbutus Ward. She's the proprietor."

"How come you live in a boardinghouse?" Peter asked.

"Panthers got 'er," Bird mumbled.

Ruby was distracted by the old man's mumbling, and did not hear Peter's question.

"Don't pay any attention to Bird," Peter said. "He rambles a lot. Has no idea what he's talking about."

"He's talking about panthers," Ruby said.

"That's right!" Bird said loudly. "There were panthers on the mountain."

"It's okay, Bird," Peter said. "There are no panthers here."

"Panthers ate her all up!" Bird cried out, pulling at his thin silver hair in agitation.

Peter comforted the old man by patting him on the back. "Who, Bird? Who did the panthers eat up?"

"Her!" Bird hollered again, pointing at Ruby.

Peter and Ruby burst into laughter. At first Bird appeared to be startled and bewildered at their amusement, but then his face melted into a sheepish grin.

"But here she is, still alive and kickin'," he admitted.

Almost immediately Bird's attention turned toward a dog on the other side of the street.

"There's old Red," he said. "Followed us all this way."

He started to cross the street, but Peter grabbed him and pulled him back.

"It's not old Red, Bird. It just looks like him."

"Did you have to leave your dog behind?" Ruby asked.

"No, we don't have a dog. Old Red was Bird's dog sixty years ago, when he was a little boy."

Busy Street, true to its name, was bustling with people, which was usual for a Saturday evening into late night, when everybody and his kin came into Way Down from the hills. They came to town to shop for supplies and to find entertainment.

Folks walked by the storefronts in pairs or small bunches, chattering, laughing, counting their coins, licking ice cream cones. Children darted in and out among the grownups.

Although it was still daylight, the Silver Screen marquee was lit up with flashing lights, advertising Alan Ladd in *Shane*. For the second feature, Gene Autry's *Riders in the Sky* was back by popular demand.

The Morgans' oldest boy, Jude, was standing in line for tickets, with Lantha Bevins hanging on to his arm, her summer cold apparently all dried up.

Beside the movie theater stood the town's only tavern,

The Beer Barrel, from which the sounds of raucous laughter and a screeching jukebox spilled carelessly onto the street.

Just beyond The Beer Barrel, the eleven-year-old identical Fuller triplets were standing on stacks of pop crates, preaching the Gospel.

Connie Lynn, Sunny Gaye, and Bonnie Clare Fuller had eyes like violets and long yellow hair, which was plaited into pigtails. This evening they were dressed alike in blue homemade sundresses and sandals. Only their parents and a few friends, including Ruby, could tell one girl from another.

The triplets had been called at an early age to preach on the streets of Way Down. At the moment they were sermonizing to people who were in the throes of real temptation, imposed on them by the rowdy tavern. A crowd had gathered to hear the girls preach. As they were wrapping up the sermon, Ruby, Peter, and Bird joined their flock.

"And the Lord said to Aaron, 'Drink no wine nor strong drink, you nor your sons with you, when you go into the tent of meeting,'" Bonnie Clare preached, slapping the Bible in her hands and emphasizing her last three words, "Lest you die!"

Then, with pigtails swinging, Sunny Gaye took her turn. "Wine is a mocker, strong drink a brawler," she cried out, "and whoever is led astray by it is not wise!"

Next Connie Lynn evangelized, "And he will drink no

wine nor strong drink, and he will be filled with the Holy Spirit!"

As if by a miracle from God himself the appalling music from The Beer Barrel ceased, and the triplets took advantage of the moment by singing "Mansion over the Hilltop" in three-part harmony. They sounded good enough to be on the radio, and people were obviously impressed, as they gave the girls a round of applause, whistles, and hoots.

"Go now and sin no more!" Bonnie Clare said, dismissing the crowd.

But alas, as the sisters stepped down off the pop crates, most of their congregation filed into The Beer Barrel. Peter struggled with Bird to keep him from following the crowd.

Ruby introduced everybody, and the triplets all spoke at once, which was their habit. It saved time.

"We're pleased to meet you," from Bonnie Clare.

"We heard about y'all moving here," from Sunny Gaye.

"Don't you have some brothers, Peter?" from Connie Lynn.

Peter scratched his head. He had heard only Connie. "Yeah, Cedar, Jeeter, and Skeeter."

He paused for the usual comment about the names, but the duplicates didn't say anything else. They just peered up at him with their six violet eyes, waiting for more.

"My mama loved to make things rhyme," he explained. "She was a poet in her last life."

"What does that mean?"

"In her last life?"

"Come again?"

"Well, my mama believed that life is a school," Peter explained, "and when we don't learn the lessons placed before us, we have to come back and repeat the grade. But if we do learn what we're here to learn, then we are promoted to the next grade. That's where she is now—in the next grade."

The triplets were too astonished to react. So was Ruby, but she also felt giddy. Here was a new card turned up!

"We have a little sister, too," Peter continued. "By the time Rita came along, Mama had run out of rhyming names, so she had to settle for a tongue twister."

"We're having a baptism tomorrow," Bonnie Clare informed him.

"Down at Deep Creek," Connie Lynn said.

"And we think you need baptizing real bad," added Sunny Gaye.

But Peter was rescued from more evangelizing at that moment when somebody put another nickel into the beastly jukebox. He threw up a hand to the triplets and moved on with Ruby and Bird.

9

SLIM MORGAN WAS STANDING IN FRONT OF HIS PARENTS' drugstore with a camera.

"Y'all pose for me, and I'll take your picture!" he called to Ruby, Peter, and Bird.

Actually Slim was not slim but rather pudgy. His hair was golden, his eyes a sparkling brown, and his nose freckled. No boy in town was better-looking or better-liked than the thirteen-year-old Slim.

He popped a blue flashbulb into his camera while Ruby and Peter posed. Bird did not know the meaning of the word *pose*, so he gazed upward into the night, as if he saw Gene Autry's legendary ghost riders in the sky.

Slim aimed and snapped, the flashbulb exploded, and Bird hollered, "Lordy, Lordy! I've been struck by lightnin'! I'm blinded!"

"You're okay, Bird," Peter said, rubbing his own offended eyes. "It's just a flashbulb."

After introductions Slim offered up his new camera for their inspection.

"I got it for my birthday today. It's a Brownie Hawk-eye, and it takes colored pictures. I'll show them to you when they get developed."

"Happy birthday, Slim," Ruby and Peter said together.

"How much does a camera like this cost?" Peter asked as he turned it over and over in his hands. Having seen very few cameras in his lifetime, he hardly knew what one should look like.

"About six dollars, I think."

"Wow, six dollars for a camera. Y'all must be rich," Peter said.

"Not a'tall. My mama and daddy run this drugstore here," Slim said, jerking his thumb toward the window.

MORGAN'S DRUGS

SINCE 1897

SCRIPTS, SCENTS, SUNDAES

"And we're not a bit rich. In fact, Daddy says he's so deep in debt, whenever he walks into the bank it starts to trembling."

"Hmmm," Peter mused. "I should think a drugstore would make you pretty well off."

"Well, Daddy says Mama trusts people too much, and gives credit on faith. And Mama says Daddy feels too much pity for the sick, and gives away more medicine than he sells."

"Wanna hang out with us?" Ruby asked Slim.

"Okay." Slim reclaimed the camera and hung the strap around his neck. "Y'all want some blow gum?"

"Sure," Ruby and Peter said together.

"Me too!" Bird added.

Slim dashed into the drugstore and came back out with two handfuls of Bazooka bubble gum. He passed around pieces to Ruby, Peter, and Bird, too.

"Happy birthday!" Bird said to Slim, as if he had just this minute heard the news.

"Well, thank you very much, Bird," Slim said. "And when is your birthday?"

"December first," Bird answered promptly.

"That's right, Granddaddy," Peter praised him, surprised and pleased that the old man remembered.

"What year?" Ruby asked.

"*Ev* . . . ry year," Bird said irritably. "Every gosh darn year that comes."

Slim and Ruby giggled, but Peter reminded Bird to watch his language.

After visiting several stores, and introducing Peter and Bird to more people than they could keep straight, the small group reached the bus depot. From there, Busy Street became Highway 99, with a string of private homes. So they went back the way they had come, taking turns at reading the Bazooka comics.

"How do you make a handkerchief dance?"

"How?"

"You put a little boogie in it!"

"When you step on a grape, what sound does it make?"

"What?"

"It lets out a little wine!"

Then they had a bubble-blowing contest. When Bird blew the biggest bubble of them all, Slim took his picture. The bubble burst all over his stubbly face, and he giggled.

"I don't know when Bird has had so much fun," Peter said as he patted his granddaddy's shoulder with affection.

Darkness had crept in, and many stores were closing up for the day. The street was almost deserted, as people had disappeared into The Beer Barrel or the Silver Screen. Others had crossed the bridge to Railroad Street to eat at The Boxcar Grill or to rollerskate at the Round & Round, or to bowl at the Back Alley.

The night air was thick with smells of summer. Across the thoroughfare in front of the courthouse, moths could be seen flitting around the streetlamps. The curb had collected paper cups, Popsicle sticks, candy wrappers, and discarded gum. But the street sweeper would be along in a few hours, and by morning the town would be as clean and tidy as Miss Arbutus's kitchen.

Upon passing The Beer Barrel again, they spied Mr. Farmer, husband to Way Down's postmistress, tumbling out the door, too intoxicated to walk straight. It was a bad habit he had picked up in the war. Ruby and Slim knew Mr. Farmer was not a bad man. He just needed a little extra help sometimes. So they took him home to his wife.

Then Slim headed back to help close up the drugstore, and Ruby, Peter, and Bird continued toward their homes.

As they neared The Roost, Peter said, "Thanks, Ruby June, for walking around town with me. You have given me a lot to think about."

"What do you mean?"

"Well, Mama used to say nobody comes into our lives by accident. We have something to learn from everybody we meet. And I met a lot of people tonight."

"Well, come and meet one more," Ruby said. "It's our star boarder. He's writing a book about Way Down."

The three of them stepped up onto the porch of The Roost, where Mr. Crawford was sitting near a lamp, reading a newspaper and sipping his evening tea.

"Hey, Mr. Crawford," Ruby greeted him. "Meet my new friend, Peter Reeder, and his granddaddy, Bird."

"Oh, from the Virginia Reeders?" Mr. Crawford said deferentially, as though he were speaking of the Washingtons or the Jeffersons. He held out a hand first to Bird, then to Peter. "Glad to meet you both. A. H. Crawford here, at your service."

"A. H.?" Peter said. "Just initials? No name?"

"I do have two front names, but I prefer not to use them. However, since you are a newcomer, I will reveal my given name to you this once, and we will not mention it again, agreed?"

"Yessir, agreed."

"My parents christened me Adolf Hilton Crawford. At the time it was a perfectly good name."

Peter repeated the name softly, then cried out, "Oh! Adolf Hit—"

"Shhh!" Mr. Crawford shushed him quickly. "Don't say it out loud."

"Sorry," Peter said.

"During the war I started using my initials only," Mr. Crawford said. "You can understand why?"

"Of course," said Peter.

"A writer shouldn't have to be ashamed of his name," Mr. Crawford said in his melancholy way. "Perhaps before my book is published, I will change it."

10

LATER, AS SHE BRUSHED MISS ARBUTUS'S HAIR AT THE dressing table, Ruby said, "Here in Way Down, Peter Reeder puts me in mind of a white unicorn tossed in with plain old brown horses."

Miss Arbutus smiled at her in the looking glass. "Then he is handsome?"

"Oh, yes, very handsome. But he needs to go see Mr. Bevins at the barbershop and get a good haircut."

"Perhaps he hasn't the money," Miss Arbutus said.

"That's probably true," Ruby said. "His daddy is going to work at the A&P for Mayor Chambers on Monday. It could be a permanent job. Peter wants a regular job, but I told him he might start by doing odd jobs for people. He asked if he could come by here tomorrow and see if you have something for him to do, and I told him yes."

"I might have work for him," Miss Arbutus said. "A boy needs a little spending money."

"Their granddaddy's name is Bird," Ruby said. "He's a bit addled. He rambled on and on about panthers."

Miss Arbutus seemed startled. "Panthers!"

Ruby nodded, and continued talking about Peter, but after a while it appeared that Miss Arbutus was not listening to her.

"What's wrong, Miss Arbutus? You act like your mind is somewhere else."

"Oh, it's nothing. Speaking of panthers reminded me of something, that's all. It brought back a memory."

"Will you tell me about it?"

"Not tonight. It's bedtime now."

And they said good night. Ruby went to her own room and stood in front of the window to view the hills against the night sky, just as she had always done. But this time was different. This time she forgot to say to her parents, "Don't forget me. Woo-bee is right here waiting for you."

Instead she said, "I hope he likes me."

Then she crawled into bed and let the night breeze waft over her. Her eyelids fluttered and closed. A dream of panthers rose up from the depths of the night.

In the next room Miss Arbutus was having the same disturbing dream of panthers screaming through the wild hills. They drew closer and closer to her until she woke up with a gasp. She did not sleep again that night. Instead she lay awake watching daylight creep over the mountains.

She heard the five o'clock freight train come hurtling into the valley toward the Way Down station. Its heartrending shriek reverberated throughout the dew-misted hills.

The train whistle was followed by the sound of the milkman's truck as it came to a stop in front of The Roost. The glass bottles clinked against one another as the milkman, Mr. Stacey, walked under Miss Arbutus's window. Mr. Stacey murmured to Jethro as he delivered a dozen eggs, a gallon of sweet milk, a quart of buttermilk, a pint of cream, and a pound of butter. He placed them carefully in a covered basket on the small back porch.

Miss Arbutus was reminded of another warm dawn in another June. She took a few moments to savor that memory before rising to meet the new day.

Meals served at Miss Arbutus's great oak table were lively, noisy affairs, with several conversations going on at once. This morning, with some of the guests dressed for church, was no exception.

Two businessmen who had arrived last night in a Packard were discussing the state of the economy with Judge Deel, while Mrs. Thornton Elkins, Mr. Gentry, and Miss Worly were talking about the importance of an education.

Lester Horton was there for his periodic visit, and Ruby was entertaining him with anecdotes about Jethro. Miss Arbutus did not participate in any exchange, as was her habit. She was nibbling at a piece of bacon and gazing out the window.

As usual, Mr. Crawford was sleeping in and would not be up for several more hours.

Above the din, Ruby caught part of a sentence, ". . . the oldest one, Peter. Smart as a whip!"

"Where did you hear that, Mrs. Thornton Elkins?" Ruby burst into that discussion, leaving Lester Horton suspended in mid-story.

"On the telephone, dear," Mrs. Thornton Elkins trilled in her fine thin voice. "You know, I just happened to pick up the receiver and overheard part of a dialogue between Mr. Dales and Mr. Doctor."

"Smart as a whip, eh?" Miss Worly mused out loud. "Catchy expression, albeit a somewhat nonsensical one. For one must wonder, just how smart is a whip?"

Ruby noticed how, as often happened, all the separate conversations had merged into one, and everybody was tuned in to the same station now—Miss Worly and her words.

"I don't know how smart a whip is either," Ruby said. "But I think Peter Reeder really is nice and smart."

"Then you have met him, Ruby June?" said Judge Deel.

"Yeah, we walked around town together last night. And his granddaddy, too."

"And how do they like our little town?" Mrs. Thornton Elkins asked.

"Fine. Peter's gonna fit right in," Ruby said.

"What's the old man like?" asked Mr. Gentry.

"His name is Bird. He's kinda goofy, so I guess he'll fit right in, too."

Friendly chuckles followed.

At the sound of the back screen door opening and closing, all eyes went to the dining room archway to see who would come through the kitchen.

Peter Reeder himself entered the dining room.

"Oh, excuse me!" he apologized, on finding the boarders eating breakfast. His face went red. "I didn't mean to intrude . . ."

"You're not intruding a'tall," Ruby said as she went to him. "Didn't I tell you nobody has to knock at The Roost? Come to the table and have a bite with us."

"No, thanks, I . . . I couldn't," he mumbled, but his eyes passed with interest over the leavings on the table—bacon, a mound of scrambled eggs on a white platter, biscuits, a gravy bowl still half-full, a plate of sliced fruit, several jars of something rich and sweet, pitchers of milk and orange juice.

"Hey, everybody, this is Peter Reeder," Ruby said to the boarders around the table.

Mrs. Thornton Elkins was the first to coax Peter. "Do come join us, young man. We have plenty."

Miss Arbutus was already laying a clean plate for Peter beside Ruby's. She motioned for him to sit. Peter glanced at the friendly faces, smiled shyly, and moved toward the chair.

"Well, okay, thanks."

Sensing that Peter was hungry, Ruby heaped his plate high without asking him what he wanted. As he dug in with gusto, the other guests discreetly averted their eyes and picked at the remains of their food.

"Clean as a whistle!" Miss Worly was saying. "That's another term I have not heretofore examined. What could possibly be clean about a whistle, with all that spittle inside it?"

11

W E'RE ALL OUT OF HONEY, AND MISS ARBUTUS WANTS you to go with me to Way Up That-a-Way and fetch some."

Peter had finished nearly everything on the table, and the other guests had gone about their day. Now Ruby and Peter were drying dishes.

"Where to?" Peter said.

"To Way Up That-a-Way," Ruby said, pointing a finger toward the back of the house. "That's what we call the place on the top of this mountain behind us. Granny Butler and her clan have a few acres up there. She keeps bees, and everybody buys her honey."

"Okay, how do we get there?"

"There's a path that starts right behind The Roost. It takes a while to walk up there, but you'll like Granny Butler. She communicates with animals."

"For real?" Peter said.

"Yes," Ruby said. "She has knowledge nobody else

has because she understands their language, and they tell her stuff."

"Would you say she's a bit pixilated?" Peter said.

"Pixilated?" Ruby did not know the word.

"That was one of Mama's words," Peter said with a chuckle. "It means crazy, but Mama thought *pixilated* sounded much better."

"It does," Ruby agreed, "but I wouldn't call Granny Butler pixilated. I *would* call her an albino."

"A what-o?"

"An albino is a person who was born without any skin pigment," Ruby informed him. "So they have no color. Granny Butler had snow-white hair even when she was young, and her skin is pale, so she can't stand much sunlight. And her eyes are . . . well, they're kinda strange-looking. They're pinkish."

"Pink eyes? No foolin'?"

"*Sorta* pink. She'll look queer to you at first, but she's so interesting, once you get to know her, why you won't even notice her appearance."

As they spread their dish towels across the sink to dry, Miss Arbutus came out of the pantry with two burlap rucksacks. Each one had four homemade pockets, and tucked into the pockets were empty pint jars. Miss Arbutus strapped one of the packs across Ruby's back and the other across Peter's.

Miss Arbutus placed money into Ruby's hand, which Ruby tucked into her shorts pocket.

In the backyard Lester Horton was petting Jethro, but

the goat left him and darted to Ruby as soon as she appeared.

"I like your little beard," Peter said as he gave the goat's whiskers a playful tug. "How come you're not standing on top of a car today?"

"He will as soon as he's left alone," Lester said. "He'll climb up on the woodpile and step across the fence to the top of that Packard. He likes to watch people going to church."

Then Ruby and Peter said goodbye to Lester and Jethro, went out the gate, and latched it behind them to keep the goat from following.

A wooden sign was staked into the ground where the path began.

WAY UP THAT-A-WAY ↑

The path wound before them, up across the face of the mountain, and disappeared into the trees beyond. The initial climb was very steep, and they didn't talk much, but instead concentrated on pulling themselves forward.

When the worst was over, Peter said, "When we got home last night, Bird told Daddy that he saw the girl who was eaten by the panther."

Ruby laughed. "Was he still stuck on that?"

"Yeah, he was. But Daddy figured out what was bothering Bird. It seems he was remembering something that happened on Yonder Mountain a long, long time ago. There was a family living on the other side of the mountain from us, who had a whole bunch of kids. In hot weather they laid quilts out on the front porch and let the little ones sleep there. Nobody dreamed that anything could happen to them. They didn't think there were any dangerous animals still stalking those hills.

"But one night the smallest girl—her name was Jolene—vanished from the porch. The dark just swallowed her up. The other children didn't see or hear a thing. A search party was organized, and they combed the area for days, but not a trace of her was to be found. Some people on the mountain said they heard a panther the very night the girl disappeared. Nobody had known of a panther being in those parts for over fifty years, but the people said they knew that's what it was because of the way it cried. A panther screams like a woman, you know."

"I've heard tell that," Ruby said.

"So everybody figured little Jolene had been devoured by a panther, just like Bird said last night."

"How awful!" Ruby said, shivering in the bright sunlight.

"Yeah, I guess it really worried Bird. He had met the girl, and he never quite got over it. Maybe you reminded him of her in some way."

They paused and looked down at the town below them, nestled in its pocket between the hills. Sure enough, at The Roost they could see Jethro standing on top of the Packard, probably chewing his cud, as he watched the people going to worship, some walking, some in cars.

"It looks like a picture in a storybook," Peter said.

"Yes, it does," Ruby agreed. "Did you know there's a treasure buried somewhere down there?"

"What kind of treasure?"

"A pirate's treasure. Gold doubloons and pieces of eight."

"No kidding?"

"That's what Miss Arbutus told me. She's a direct descendant of the man who settled this town—Archibald Ward the first. He's the one who buried the treasure."

As they continued their hike, church bells from the three churches in the valley began ringing. Almost immediately one dog in town started howling like an old hound hot on a trail. Following his lead, all the other dogs, one by one, began to howl as well. Their chorus grew so loud, you could barely make out the sound of the bells. Ruby and Peter looked at each other and smiled. The day felt good, perfect.

As they crossed over a treeless patch of the mountain, there were wildflowers growing by the path, and blackberry blossoms everywhere. Ruby thought it would be a dandy spot for a picnic next month during berry season.

"Don't you belong to a church?" Peter interrupted her thoughts.

"No, but I sometimes attend the services here or there. In warm weather I like to go to evening vespers," Ruby said. "We meet outside under the stars. I love to sing out of doors in the dark. You can hear the voices echoing against the mountainside."

The dogs had finally settled down, and Ruby and Peter paused to enjoy the bells.

"Speaking of echoes," Peter said, "that name—you know the name Mr. A. H. Crawford said we should not mention? Well, I dreamed I was in a cave, and that name kept echoing off the walls. Where was he this morning? In his room writing?"

"No, he was sleeping," Ruby said. "He hardly ever opens his eyes before noon. I think Mr. Crawford has missed a lot because he has never seen a sunrise."

"Never?"

"*Probably* never. Sad people seem to need a lot of sleep."

"How many hours do you think he sleeps?"

"It's hard to say," Ruby said. "He gets up and goes to The Boxcar Grill for dinner, and he might take a nap before supper. He has a record player, and he plays the same sad song over and over. He goes to his room around nine or so at night. Then he probably reads for a while."

"When does he write?" Peter wanted to know. "I'm anxious to read his book."

Ruby shrugged and did not answer his question. Instead she said, "Miss Arbutus says that sleep is more important for the soul than for the body. She says when a person sleeps a lot like Mr. Crawford does, they are trying to work out their problems."

"And how does sleeping help?"

"Because, according to Miss Arbutus," Ruby said, "God is in that place where sleep takes us. Way down deep inside, where all the answers lie."

12

"**!!^^##**!!~~**!!"

Ruby had heard a few bad words in her day, but nothing to compare with this string of offensive language coming from somewhere on the trail behind them. It made her ears burn.

She and Peter were approaching a clearing at the top of the mountain, where a patch of new corn was growing. Now they stopped to look back at a clump of scrubby trees they had just passed under.

"Uh-oh," Peter said glumly. "I should have known he would follow me."

"Who?" Ruby said.

At that moment a barefooted, shorter version of Peter appeared on the path. He was tugging angrily at his clothing.

"**!!^^##**!!~~**!!" He repeated his litany.

"Cedar!" Peter scolded him. "Will you watch your language? There's a nice girl here."

"It's these **!! beggar-lice!" Cedar shot back. "They are all over my britches!"

He came up beside Peter and Ruby, pulling the prickly burrs off his raggedy pants. "And every **##!! time I pull two off, three more pop up someplace else!"

"What are you doing here?" Peter asked heatedly.

"Pulling off these @@**!! beggar-lice!" Cedar replied. "What are you doing?"

The two brothers stood facing each other, both seeming plumb put out.

"Who is looking after Bird and the kids?" Peter asked.

"Daddy, that's who."

"You should be helping him," Peter scolded.

"And so should you!" Cedar responded. "You slipped off from me last night, and I didn't say a **!! word. So I was hoping you'd ask me to go with you today. Why didn't you?"

"Because I don't want to hear your mouth!" Peter said angrily. "You embarrass me with your cussing!"

"Maybe I won't cuss today," Cedar said nonchalantly as he looked Ruby up and down. "Who are you?"

Ruby opened her lips to answer, but Peter stopped her by saying, "We're not going to tell you until you promise! *Maybe* is not good enough."

"Okay," Cedar agreed sulkily.

"Okay what?" Peter said.

"I promise."

"This is Ruby June," Peter said grumpily. "Ruby June, my brother Cedar."

"I know she's not your sweetheart," Cedar said. "She's too pretty for you."

"I oughta wop you a good one up the side of the head!" Peter hollered.

Cedar just laughed. "Where y'all going to, anyhow?"

Peter was too aggravated to answer. He continued walking, and Ruby fell in behind him, Cedar behind her.

"Where y'all going to?" Cedar repeated, but nobody answered him.

Now the corn grew on both sides of the path. Ahead of them under a giant tree sat a picturesque cabin, built from the pale wood of the surrounding hills. A slate walkway led to the front door.

Before they could reach the entrance of the cabin, the door opened, and Granny Butler stepped out, wearing a frilly apron over a blue gingham dress. She was short and thin, with skin as pallid as cream.

A pair of thick wire-rimmed spectacles balanced on Granny Butler's small nose. As they drew near her, they could see that the whites of her eyes were somewhat pink, as Ruby had said, while the irises were a very light blue.

"!!—" Cedar started to swear at sight of the lady, but instead clamped both hands over his mouth, and held them there.

Granny Butler seemed not to notice.

"Ruby June!" she said, grinning all over. "I knew you were coming!"

"How did you know, Granny Butler?"

"Aristotle told me last night when I was trying to go to sleep. He told me that somebody's coming to see me tomorrow. Then he said, 'Guess whoo? Whoo?'

"And I said to him, 'I can't imagine. Whoo? Whoo?'

"And he said back to me, "Rooo-beee Jooo-oon.' "

"But I didn't know myself until this morning," Ruby said.

"Well, what can I say? Aristotle is the wisest of the wise."

"Who's Aristotle?" Cedar wanted to know.

"He's a smart old white owl," Ruby said.

Granny Butler adjusted her glasses and squinted at the boys. "Who you got there with you?"

Ruby introduced Peter and Cedar to Granny Butler, and she motioned for the three of them to follow her around to the back of the cabin, toward the springhouse, where she kept her honey cool.

A narrow path snaked through tall tufts of broom straw and dropped out of sight over the edge of the hill. Ruby, Peter, and Cedar followed Granny Butler single file.

"And where y'all from?" she called over her shoulder to Peter and Cedar.

"Yonder Mountain in Virginia," Peter replied. "We just moved to Way Down Deep yesterday."

"Oh, I reckon it was your daddy who tried to rob the bank?"

Ruby could see Peter's ears turning red.

"He wadn't serious or nothing," Cedar explained. "He had a toy gun."

"I know it," Granny Butler said. "Ripple the red fox told me all about it. He was stealing eggs from Mayor Chambers's henhouse when he overheard the mayor and his wife through the open kitchen window, talking. Ripple got so excited, he streaked away and forgot the eggs. So he came to me begging for supper that night."

"A **!! fox told you?" Cedar cried out with disbelief. "Owls telling you stuff. Foxes talking to you. That's the stupidest thing I ever heard!"

Granny Butler came to an abrupt standstill, causing the threesome to tumble all over each other. The old woman swung her body around to face Cedar. For a long moment she gazed at him, and Cedar seemed to wilt like a morning glory at high noon.

"Young man, you are going to meet somebody," Granny Butler said to him, "who will set you straight about your bad mouth. And you will be wise to listen."

Then she went on as if nothing had happened. Cedar followed with his chin on his chest.

Granny Butler's springhouse was located down in a small hollow under a cluster of trees. When she opened the door, a whiff of cold air rose up from inside, laden with the odor of wet earth and toadstools. She carefully descended three broken steps and tiptoed around the edge of the spring inside.

"How much you want today?" she said to Ruby.

"Eight pints," Ruby said.

"I'll reach them up to you," Granny Butler said, "so you won't have to come down in here."

She took a pint of honey from a shelf in the wall and handed it up the steps.

"The bees send their greetings. They made this special for Ruby June. And lucky for you, I'm running a sale this week—buy one, get one free."

"That's good news," Ruby said as she removed an empty jar from Peter's rucksack and replaced it with the full one. "A quarter a pint, right?"

"Oh, no," Granny replied, as she peeped around the doorframe, holding the second jar. "I had to go up to fifty cents a pint. That's the only way I can afford to run a buy-one-get-one-free sale."

As Granny Butler ducked back inside for another jar, Ruby and Peter looked at each other. They both smiled, then looked away quickly and bit their lips to keep from laughing out loud.

Cedar sat down on a rock to watch. Ruby loaded honey into the pockets of the rucksack on Peter's back. When his pack was full, Peter began to fill Ruby's.

At last Ruby and Peter had four pints each, and the empty jars lay on the ground. Granny Butler would clean them and refill them with honey. Granny Butler came out of the springhouse, and Ruby gave the honey money to her.

"Thank you, Ruby June. You can tell Miss Arbutus I appreciate her business, and pretty soon I'm gonna start making and selling molasses."

"Okay. How much will you charge for it?"

"One pint for thirty cents, three pints for a dollar."

13

AFTER ENJOYING A COLD GLASS OF BUTTERMILK WITH
Granny Butler on her front porch, Ruby, Peter, and
Cedar said goodbye to her and started back the way they
had come.

But before they had gone far, Granny Butler called
out, "Ruby June, let me have a private word with you."

"Go ahead," Ruby said to the brothers. "I'll catch up."

The two boys continued toward the corn patch.

"Aristotle told me something else about you," Granny
Butler said softly to Ruby when they were alone.

"Really? What?"

"He said, and I quote, 'The mystery of Ruby June is
about to unravel.'"

Ruby's blue eyes grew round and large. "No! He
didn't!"

"Yes, he did. I would not tell you a lie."

"Oh, I know you wouldn't. I'm . . . well, shocked, surprised. I don't know how to take it."

"Just take it as it comes, and don't let it worry your pretty head," Granny Butler said.

"How does Aristotle know so much?"

"He is older than the hills, and he knows everybody and remembers everything."

"Is that all he said?"

"To tell you the truth, Ruby June, getting information from Aristotle is like trying to eat soup with a fork. Just ever' once in a while he gives you a morsel. He wouldn't say more than that, but he did say he heard it all from a panther."

"A panther! There aren't any panthers in these hills!"

"No, but there usta be, my girl. There usta be."

Granny Butler abruptly disappeared into her cabin, leaving Ruby alone, her mind racing with questions. She hurried along the path through the corn, only to find Peter and Cedar quarreling.

"**!!^^##**!!~~**!!" Cedar was hollering.

So much for promises.

Later Ruby could not recall much of the trip back down the mountain. She did vaguely remember Peter asking her once more why she lived in a boardinghouse, but she said she didn't feel like talking about it.

"It's okay," Peter said quickly. "Some things are personal, and I didn't mean to get nosy."

Back in the kitchen of The Roost, Miss Arbutus unstrapped the rucksack from Ruby's back, then Peter's. Cedar had stayed outside. Peter was saying goodbye at the door when Miss Arbutus tried to press a quarter into his hand.

"No, ma'am," he objected. "After that big breakfast I can't take money from you."

Finally he agreed to take one pint of honey home to his family, and he was gone. Ruby felt a moment of regret that their time together was over, but she couldn't think of that right now because Granny Butler's words were going around and around in her head.

The mystery of Ruby June is about to unravel.

Miss Arbutus was studying her face. "What is it, Ruby June?"

"Just a headache," Ruby said. It was true that her head had started to hurt. "Too much sun."

She went to her room and lay down on the yellow-and-white ruffled bed. The pansy curtains moved slightly with the breeze, and outside she could hear some small children playing May I? on the sidewalk. She was reminded of past days when she was just a child herself playing that game. There were many such sweet memories of growing up in this fine old house with Miss Arbutus.

"Take two baby steps."

"May I?"

"Yes, you may."

"Take a giant step."

The mystery of Ruby June is about to unravel.

"Uh-oh! You forgot to say *May I?* You have to go all the way back to the start line."

Heard it from a panther.

"What am I afraid of?" Ruby asked herself. "Haven't I always wanted to know who I am, where I came from? Why else did I think of my parents all those nights and say to them, 'Don't forget me. Woo-bee is right here waiting for you'?"

Sometimes she did feel like she was waiting for someone to come and get her. Someone who had just gone to the store or to the movies, leaving Miss Arbutus to babysit.

What would it be like to have a father? Some fathers were strict. Would he boss her around? Would he change everything?

She thought of the woman in the rocking chair who had haunted her in the wee hours of so many mornings. Yes, she had felt secure and loved when that woman was near because she was sure it was her mother, but now she felt threatened. Someone might take her away from all that she had grown to love. That was why she was afraid.

Later, as they manicured their nails, Ruby debated with herself about telling Miss Arbutus what Granny Butler had said. It would be nice to share it, she thought, but then again, maybe this was Granny Butler's imagination working overtime. Already the news had given Ruby a headache, so why worry Miss Arbutus with it?

14

THE NEXT DAY, AFTER COMPLETING HER ERRANDS, RUBY was pulling the Radio Flyer up Busy Street toward home when she met Cedar Reeder walking in front of the doctors' office.

"Hey there, Cedar!" she greeted him. "Where's Peter?"

"Oh, he's looking after Bird and the kids. Daddy started working for Mayor Chambers today at the A&P."

"And what are you up to?" she asked him.

"I was just walking down Ward Street minding my own business when this real old woman tried to kill me."

"What!"

"I'm not foolin'. Lookee here!"

Cedar pulled his T-shirt aside, revealing a small red spot on his shoulder.

"That **##~~ old hag hit me with a rock, and I didn't do a thing to her!"

"It was only Mrs. Rife," Ruby said. "She throws itty-bitty rocks. They don't hurt much."

"Well, I'm gonna throw one back at her next time!" Cedar declared.

"Cedar! Don't you dare!" Ruby scolded him. "She's ninety years old!"

"I don't give a—"

But Cedar did not get a chance to finish because someone interrupted by yelling, "Hey there, Ruby June! Who're you talking to?"

It was Reese Mullins, pushing a cart full of fresh produce across the street. He had been selling it in the residential areas, and now to people on Busy Street. This was one of Reese's jobs when The Boxcar Grill became overrun with vegetables and fruits.

"Hey, Reese," she greeted him. "This is Cedar Reeder, one of the new boys."

"Is he the one you were stepping out with on Saturday night?" Reese demanded to know.

"I was not 'stepping out,' as you put it, with anybody!" Ruby said hotly.

"That was my brother Peter," Cedar contributed.

"My name is Reese Mullins," Reese said, "and you can tell your brother Peter that Ruby June is *my* girlfriend."

"Now, Reese Mullins, you are telling a big fat lie," Ruby scolded. "I am not your girlfriend or anybody else's."

"Well," Reese said sulkily, "if you was anybody's girlfriend, you'd be mine, now wouldn't you?"

Ruby was embarrassed and desperately wanted the topic of conversation changed. Luckily her eye fell on a poster in the doctors' window. It was a notice about Kids' Day.

"They have started advertising about Kids' Day already," she said to Cedar, eagerly pointing to the ad.

"What's Kids' Day?" Cedar asked.

"It's a day at the end of the summer when all the businesses give things free to kids. And we have a parade, a carnival, a free movie, free bowling and skating, all the pop and candy and ice cream we can hold, and I don't know what all."

"What's it for?" Cedar said.

"Just to show appreciation for the kids in town."

"Can I go with you and Peter on Kids' Day?" Cedar asked.

"She always goes with me!" Reese blurted out.

"Everybody goes together!" Ruby snapped at Reese. Then she turned her back to him as she talked to Cedar. "You and Peter must bring your twin brothers and your little sister, too."

Reese was doing a slow burn. Here was this new kid, younger than he was, by cracky, getting more attention from Ruby than she had ever given to him.

"I can sing!" Reese blurted out. "I always sing to Ruby June, don't I, Ruby June?"

Ruby rolled her eyes, then turned to face Reese again. "Don't sing, Reese, please?" she pleaded with him.

"It's 'Push Cart Serenade,' " Reese informed Cedar. "I learned it from the radio so I could sing it to Ruby June when I'm selling my fruits and vegetables."

Ruby groaned, knowing what she was in for, but she had learned there was no stopping Reese. He began to sing "Push Cart Serenade."

"BEETS! BEETS!
How my heart beats for you.
BEETS! BEETS!
Say yours beats for me too.
LETTUCE!
Oh, LETTUCE! get married today.
HONEYDEW! HONEYDEW!
Say you're mine to stay, hey!
PEARS! PEARS!
We'd make a lovely pair.
PEACHES! PEACHES!
The peachiest anywhere.
If we CANTALOUPE! CANTALOUPE!
How I will pine.
Oh, ORANGE! you gonna be mine?"

Cedar groaned, for Reese was without a doubt the worst singer he had ever heard.

Then suddenly from out of nowhere another person had joined them on the sidewalk, and was now saying, "Reese Mullins, I want to buy some of your vegetables!"

It was Mrs. Bevins. "That is, if you can stop courting long enough to tend your business."

But Reese doggedly went on with his song to the end.

"If you CARROT! all, CARROT! all, please marry me.
We'll get by on my CELERY!"

Then he grinned and made a wide, sweeping bow to Ruby, while Mrs. Bevins stood by impatiently tapping her black high heels on the sidewalk. Wearing canary yellow trimmed in black, she had outdone herself this day. One's eye was naturally drawn first to the lemon yellow skirt, where there were wide bands of black at equal intervals. Underneath she was obviously wearing several stiff crinolines, which made the skirt stand out like an umbrella. As always, Mrs. Bevins's eyelids were decorated with shadow, and today she had chosen black. On top of her head was a yellow beany-type hat with two thin black feathers resembling antennae.

"##**!!," Cedar suddenly bellowed, pointing to Mrs. Bevins's outfit. "You look like a **!! bumblebee!"

After a quick examination of Mrs. Bevins's outfit, Ruby felt an unholy giggle trying to escape from her throat. Tactfully, she managed to swallow it, but not so with Cedar. He had about as much tact as a wild animal.

"Just look at her!" he squealed gleefully. "A ##!!** bumblebee!"

At first Mrs. Bevins was too stunned to react. She simply stood there, her face glowing pink, then red, then burgundy. Unfortunately, at that moment she caught her reflection in the doctors' window, and a giant bumblebee looked back at her. Abruptly Mrs. Bevins made an about-face in her snappy heels and stalked away with crinolines swishing and antennae bobbing.

15

REESE AND RUBY WERE SPEECHLESS. THEY LOOKED AT each other, horrified, and not a word came to mind.

All this time, unobserved by anyone, Mr. Doctor had been standing behind the screen of his waiting room door, watching and listening to the children. He chose this moment to poke his head out.

"Young man," he said to Cedar, "I am a doctor, and I'm afraid you have a serious condition. You must come into my office at once!"

Cedar touched a finger to his chest. "Who, me?"

"Yes, you."

"What! I ain't sick. What the **!! is wrong with you?"

"I must insist that you come in here immediately!" the doctor said more forcefully.

Cedar looked at Reese and Ruby and jerked one thumb toward the doctor. "Is he pixilated?"

"No, he's Presbyterian," Reese said.

Mr. Doctor was holding the screen door open wide.

Cedar hesitated, then shuffled toward him. Inside, the waiting room was empty.

"Come into my private office," Mr. Doctor said to him as he stepped to the right.

The drone of a dentist drill could be heard from the left, where Mrs. Doctor's office was located. Cedar did not like that sound at all, so he hurried along behind Mr. Doctor. When they were in Mr. Doctor's office, he motioned for Cedar to sit in a chair, where he listened to the boy's heart with a stethoscope.

"Just what I was afraid of," the doctor said after a few moments. "It's weighing your heart down."

"What are you talking about?" Cedar cried, his face turning almost as red as Mrs. Bevins's. "There's nothing wrong with me."

"Of course there is! You have the worst case of cussitis I have ever heard."

"Of what?!"

"Cussitis, a most severe case, and we must treat it promptly before it gets any worse, or before it spreads. It's extremely contagious."

"There ain't no such disease!" Cedar argued loudly.

"Who's the doctor here anyway?" Mr. Doctor said sternly. "I know cussitis when I see it. It is caused by two very dangerous germs—pain and anger. And these germs attack the vocabulary so that the afflicted person is not able to express his true feelings."

Cedar studied the doctor with narrowed eyes, but didn't react.

"I recommend four steps to recovery," the doctor said. "First, you should find some things that belonged to your mother. Touch them. Smell them. Second, talk to your father about how you feel."

"We don't talk about that!" Cedar yelled angrily.

"Oh, my, it's worse than I thought," Mr. Doctor said with concern in his voice. "You *must* talk about it, and you must do it right away!"

"You're just a **^^## crazy old man!" Cedar hollered, but his eyes were beginning to fill with tears.

"Good! Good!" the doctor praised him. "Crying is the third step. A good hard cry."

"I ain't crying!" Cedar screamed with anger. "Boys don't cry!"

"I beg to differ," Mr. Doctor said. "Boys certainly do cry! I cried my eyes out when *my* mother died. And as a result, I destroyed those dangerous germs—pain and anger. I drowned them with my tears."

But Cedar held his own tears in check.

"It does no good to swallow your feelings," Mr. Doctor kindly advised him. "They will continue to plague you in offensive ways."

At that, Cedar Reeder bolted from the doctor's office and back onto the street, where Ruby and Reese were still standing as he had left them.

"Dumb old doctor!" Cedar cried as he raced past them. "***@@@!!!*** old quack!"

16

AFTER DINNER THAT EVENING, RUBY SKIPPED UP THE sidewalk toward the house where the Reeders now lived. It was a nice summer evening.

Peter and Cedar were on the spacious front porch with Bird when she arrived. Bird was in a rocking chair, his ankle bells jingling softly every time he rocked. The boys were sitting on stools. All were stringing green beans into pans.

Peter's face lit up when he saw her. "Oh, hi there, Ruby June!"

"Hi, Peter, Cedar, Bird!" Ruby said as she stepped up onto the porch. "I came to meet the rest of the family."

Ruby was itching to know what Mr. Doctor had said to Cedar, but she didn't like to meddle unless she had to. Perhaps Cedar would volunteer the information. She could only hope.

Hearing a voice through the screen door, the twins came out, with Robber Bob behind them. In the dim light one might mistake the short man for one of the kids.

"My twin brothers, Jeeter and Skeeter," Peter said. "Jeeter is the one on the left, and Skeeter . . ."

The identical twins laughed.

Peter started all over. "Jeeter is the one on the right."

The twins laughed again as they traded places.

"Well anyway," Peter went on, "this is Daddy."

"I remember you from the bank," Robber Bob said to Ruby.

"And sneaking up behind you, Ruby June, is our little Rita," Peter said fondly. "She was trying to catch a lightning bug."

Ruby felt a small hand slip itself into one of her own. She looked around and down into the sweet face of five-year-old Rita Reeder. The child smiled up at her, showing a deep dimple in each cheek. Like the other children, she had Robber Bob's wide gray eyes. But she was wearing a ragged brown shirt and shorts that subdued her natural brightness.

Ruby remembered what Robber Bob had said about Rita—that she had not spoken a word since her mother died. She placed an arm around Rita's thin shoulders.

"I've been wanting to meet you, Rita," she said.

"Come have a seat, Ruby June," Peter said to her as he cleaned off another wooden stool beside his.

Ruby went to sit down, and Rita followed, still clinging tightly to her hand, as if she feared it might be snatched from her.

"She craves the feminine touch," Robber Bob said softly. "She attaches herself to every female person that comes along."

"Then we should be friends," Ruby said to Rita. "If you want to, you can go with me on my round of errands tomorrow on Busy Street. Would you like that?"

Rita nodded eagerly.

"I'll come by and get you right after breakfast, and you can ride in my red wagon, okay?"

The child's eyes were bright as she nodded again, and smiled. She stood very close to Ruby.

Each member of the Reeder family watched this exchange carefully, pleased at Ruby's attention to the child.

"Won't that be fun, Rita?" Jeeter or Skeeter said to her.

Rita beamed as her head bobbed up and down.

"You can come back home and tell us all about it," Robber Bob said.

"Panthers ate her all up," Bird said suddenly.

"Don't start, Bird!" Peter said with annoyance.

"She was a little bitty thing," Bird went on doggedly.

"What the **## are you talking about?" Cedar screeched.

"Watch your mouth!" Robber Bob snapped at him.

"He's talking about that girl who was grabbed by a panther on Yonder Mountain," Peter said.

"Ate her all up," Bird said again.

"Now, Dad," Robber Bob said, laying a hand on the old man's shoulder. "Don't think about that right now."

"Redheaded," Bird said.

"Yes, that girl, Jolene Hurley, was redheaded, too, just like Ruby June. Lots of people have red hair."

"Real real red, real real curly," Bird said.

"You're real real crazy!" Cedar mumbled.

"Just a little bitty thing," Bird went on.

And to everybody's surprise, Bird started to cry. Nobody spoke for a moment. Robber Bob began massaging the old man's shoulders. "What's the matter, Dad? It's not a bit like you to act up the way you're doing."

Bird continued to cry, and one of the twins removed the pan of green beans from his lap.

Peter spoke tenderly to his grandfather. "Does Ruby June remind you of the girl?"

Bird nodded. "She favors Jolene," he managed to say.

Rita went to Bird and leaned her head against him, but he could not be comforted.

"Come on, Dad, you're tired, let's get you to bed," Robber Bob said as he helped the old man to his feet.

Bird did not object. Meekly, he allowed Robber Bob to lead him into the house. Unlike the flighty Bird of Saturday night, this stooped-over, gray-headed man seemed very old and worn out.

"I don't know what y'all are talking about," Cedar said to Peter, when the two men were gone inside.

"Me either," Jeeter or Skeeter whispered. "Who got eat up by a panther?"

Rita returned to Ruby, and the twins sat down on the top step, as Peter, in low tones, told the story he had heard from his father.

"When the ***!!! did that happen?" Cedar asked.

"Watch your mouth!" Peter said. "A long, long time ago. When Bird was a boy, I think."

"Oh, no, not that long ago," Robber Bob said, as he rejoined the group after tucking the old man into bed. "Now, let me think . . ."

Robber Bob leaned against a post, scratched his chin, and looked at the evening sky.

"Was it when you were a boy, Daddy?" Jeeter or Skeeter asked him.

"No, it wadn't that long ago either. It was . . . I remember it was warm. It was . . . yeah, that was it! It was around your birthday, Peter—your third birthday, as a matter of fact.

"Cedar was just a tiny thing, and after the sorry events of that night, me and Pearl wouldn't let you two out of sight. We didn't talk about it in front of y'all either, 'cause for one thing we didn't want you to be scared of the dark, and for another it was too awful to tell it to young'uns."

"Around my third birthday? No foolin'?" Peter said.

"Yeah, that's right," Robber Bob said. "I remember it well. Now, what year would that be?"

"Nineteen forty-four," Peter said.

"That's right," Robber Bob agreed. "It was June of 1944."

17

RUBY DID NOT REACT. SHE SAT IN STONY SILENCE WHILE the Reeders lightened up the conversation with funny things that had happened in their family.

Rita had captured Ruby's hand again. Somewhere Ruby found a smile and pasted it onto her face, but she did not participate in the conversation.

"Who was it that taught his dog to use the outhouse?" Cedar was saying.

"Was it Uncle Wick?" Skeeter or Jeeter said.

"Yeah, it sure was," Peter said with a laugh. "It was Uncle Wick. That dog would stand at the outhouse door and bark when he wanted to go."

They all laughed, even little Rita. Ruby's smile stayed in place.

"Yeah, Ruby June, my brother, Wick, was a card," Robber Bob said. "A true hillbilly. One time he met up with a dandy from Richmond who talked real proper, you know, like he had a big education. So Wick asked that city slicker, 'Where'd you go to school at?'

"And the city slicker said, 'Yale.'

"So Wick hollered in his ear, '*Where'd you go to school at?*' "

Robber Bob and his children cracked up. Ruby refreshed the plastic smile, but her face was beginning to ache. When their laughter died down, she jumped to her feet so abruptly, her wooden stool toppled over. She did not bother to pick it up.

"I'm afraid I have to go now." She rushed through the words. "I have to get ready for bed."

Rita grabbed her around the waist.

"It's just barely dark," Skeeter or Jeeter protested.

But Ruby did not seem to hear. She bent over and looked into Rita's face. "I won't forget you in the morning," she said.

"I'll walk you home," Peter offered, and stood up.

"Oh, no!" Ruby said firmly. "No. I . . . I'll be seeing you!"

She unwound herself from Rita's embrace and was down the steps and out of sight in a jiffy. The Reeders looked at one another with questions in their eyes.

"Did we say something wrong?" Peter said.

"Don't blame it on me. I didn't cuss much," Cedar said.

"She did act kinda funny, didn't she?" Robber Bob said as he picked up Ruby's stool and straddled it. Then he shrugged. "Well, maybe she's not fond of hillbilly jokes."

Ruby slowed her pace as she came near The Roost.

She could see Mr. Crawford sitting on the front porch, staring into the night in his dark, brooding way. He had run an extension cord, as he often did, from the common room to his phonograph, which was on a table beside him. Of course, he was playing the same song he always played.

Miss Worly and Mr. Gentry came out together, exchanged a few words with Mr. Crawford, then headed toward Busy Street. They were probably going to the movies.

Ruby reached the porch, stepped up, and saw Mrs. Thornton Elkins through the window, curled up on the couch with the phone to her ear, listening in on the party line.

I don't have to do anything! Ruby thought. *I can go on here as if nothing was ever said! They will forget all about it, and I will never tell!*

"Everybody is haunted by somebody," Mr. Crawford was saying to her. "Who haunts you, Ruby June?"

Ruby did not answer. She was tuned in to the other sounds of the house. From an open window on the third floor she could hear the circuit-riding evangelist, who had arrived during the afternoon, practicing his sermon for the tent revival. From the laundry room Miss Arbutus's sewing machine was whirring like a hummingbird.

"It's my mother who haunts me," Mr. Crawford went on. "She gave me away when I was a baby."

Jolted back to the moment, Ruby turned to face Mr. Crawford.

"But I've heard you talk about your parents," she said.

"Oh, yes, my adopted family," Mr. Crawford said. "They're dead now. They were wonderful to me. They gave me everything—plenty of love, care, money. But all my life it has been my real mother I've searched for everywhere in every stranger's face."

Ruby was stunned.

"The adoption records are sealed for all time," Mr. Crawford went on. "I don't even know what her name was. But I call her Laura. The first time I heard this song, I named my mother that. Listen."

Ruby tilted an ear toward the spinning record, and listened to the words of Mr. Crawford's favorite song. To her surprise he began to sing along softly, and his voice was not bad.

> "Laura is the face in the misty light,
> Footsteps that you hear down the hall.
> The laugh that floats on a summer night,
> That you can never quite recall.
> And you see Laura
> On a train that is passing through.
> Those eyes, how familiar they seem.
> She gave your very first kiss to you.
> That was Laura! But she's only a dream."

"How can a mother give away a child?" Ruby whispered to the night.

"What's that?" Mr. Crawford said.

"Do you think my mother gave me away?" she asked in a strained voice.

"Oh, no! No, Ruby June." Mr. Crawford was immediately jarred from his self-pitying mood. "I did not mean that. I have no more idea than you do . . . than anybody does, how you happened to . . ."

He did not go on.

"How a toddler happened to appear in a strange town all alone?" Ruby said.

"That's right," Mr. Crawford said. "People in Way Down have pondered this mystery for years. There is no logical explanation for it."

"If she gave me away . . . if she came here and dumped me, then she did not care, and would probably not want me back now, would she?" said Ruby.

Mr. Crawford searched for the right words.

"But if she did *not* give you away, Ruby. If you were taken from her, kidnapped, stolen—which is possible, you know—then she may have been searching for you all these years. I . . . I feel sure she loved you."

Mr. Crawford replaced the needle at the beginning of the record. As Ruby listened, she clutched at that wisp of a memory she had, of being rocked beside a window, through which she could see snow falling. She could almost see the face of the woman who held her . . . almost, but not quite.

. . . the face in the misty light . . .
That you can never quite recall . . .

The song was too heavy, too sad, too close to her own situation. Ruby bolted into the house. She found Miss Arbutus at her sewing machine. Beside her, on a worktable, was a small, colorful pile of Ruby's underpants. Miss Arbutus glanced up and smiled as Ruby entered.

"What are you doing?" Ruby said in a tremulous voice.

Miss Arbutus did not notice. "I'm putting new elastic in your day-of-the-week step-ins. I've already done Tuesday, Wednesday, Thursday, and Friday. I'll finish before I turn in."

"I have something to tell you," Ruby said.

This time Miss Arbutus heard Ruby's troubled tone. Instantly she put aside her sewing and stood up. "Let's go into my room."

Together they went in and sat down on Miss Arbutus's huge, old-fashioned iron bed. In a soft clear voice, Ruby repeated what Robber Bob had said. Miss Arbutus listened to every word, but did not herself speak.

"June of 1944," Ruby finished.

Miss Arbutus placed an arm around Ruby. Her face was anxious, but still she did not speak.

"And Bird said she was a tiny thing—a little red-headed, curly-headed girl. It's an amazing coincidence, don't you think?" Ruby whispered.

"Do you know where Yonder Mountain is?" Miss Arbutus spoke at last.

"No, just somewhere in Virginia. Don't you know?"

"No."

They sat in silence for what seemed like a long time.

"Do you want to pursue this matter, Ruby June?" Miss Arbutus finally said.

"Pursue it in what way?"

"Maybe tell the sheriff."

"And then what?"

"I don't know. That would be up to him."

After a long pause, Ruby said, "I'll sleep on it."

Quietly and thoughtfully they went about their evening ritual of bathing, brushing their teeth and hair, and slathering their limbs with lotion.

As they manicured their nails, Ruby told Miss Arbutus about Granny Butler and the prediction made by Aristotle. The room was so quiet, you could hear the night bugs flying against the screen window.

"I need a hug tonight," Ruby told Miss Arbutus before going to her room.

"And so do I," Miss Arbutus said as she folded her long arms around the girl. Then they stood together in a warm embrace, both feeling comforted.

18

WELL, I SLEPT ON IT," RUBY SAID TO MISS ARBUTUS as she came in to help with breakfast.

"And?" Miss Arbutus urged her to go on.

"And I didn't get any answers, but I feel better. So let's give it to the sheriff. Let him deal with it, okay?"

Miss Arbutus didn't answer.

"Oh, I know you don't like to go to Busy Street," Ruby said. "So I'll go by myself after I've finished my errands."

To Ruby's surprise, Miss Arbutus said, "I'll meet you there."

After breakfast, Ruby went to pick up Rita Reeder, as she had promised. Robber Bob had gone to work already, but the rest of the family saw Rita off in the Radio Flyer.

Rita's face was shining, but Ruby was sorry to see that the child was dressed in the same ratty outfit she had worn the night before. She made a mental note to ask Miss Arbutus about clothes for Rita. She knew that many of her own outgrown clothes were tucked away in the attic. Miss Arbutus never got rid of anything.

"First we're going to Morgan's Drugs for aspirin and Band-Aids," Ruby said as she walked down the sidewalk, pulling the wagon with Rita in it. "Then we're going to the A&P for vanilla flavoring and baking powder and peanut butter, and . . . and . . . something else. It's on my list." She patted her pocket. "Your daddy will be there working. Then we're going to the courthouse to see the sheriff."

It was a beautiful morning, and Busy Street was full of activity, with people going to work, or running errands. Rita began to flash her dimples and wave at people on the street, and they all smiled back, or stopped to speak. When Ruby introduced them to Rita, the child never spoke, but she didn't stop smiling.

Everybody in the drugstore had to pat Rita on the head or pinch her rosy cheeks.

"What a charmer!"

"Bless her little heart!"

"No bigger'n a minute, is she?"

Ruby was reminded of the days when she was small and Miss Arbutus took her places she had to go. People had been just as attentive to her, and she remembered Miss Arbutus standing aside quietly, beaming with pride, as if Ruby were her own child.

Robber Bob was in the back of the grocery store in the meat section, trying to learn how to cut pork chops without slicing off a finger. He didn't have time to visit with Ruby and Rita, but he waved and smiled.

At the courthouse, where the sheriff's office was located on the first floor, Ruby parked the wagon outside with all the items she had bought in it. It was a common belief among Way Down folks that anybody who would steal must be in great need, so they should help themselves. Rarely did anything go missing.

When Ruby entered the sheriff's office, holding Rita by the hand, Miss Arbutus was already there, sitting quietly in a wingback chair, her hands folded before her. The five-year-old left Ruby, walked straight to Miss Arbutus, and climbed onto her lap.

"She takes to you like a fly to flypaper!" Ruby exclaimed.

Surprised though she was, Miss Arbutus's face showed that she was pleased. She placed an arm around Rita and smiled into the dimpled face. Rita leaned her head contentedly against her.

For the past five or ten minutes the sheriff had found himself in the awkward position of trying to think up things to say to Miss Arbutus. She had responded only with a smile, a nod, or a yes or no.

"Ruby June!" he said, with relief in his voice. "So glad you're here. Miss Arbutus said you have something to tell me, but that's all I could get out of her."

"She doesn't like to talk," Ruby said. "But she tells me that I talk enough for the both of us."

The sheriff chuckled.

When Ruby finished telling the sheriff Robber Bob's story, she waited for him to react, but he just sat there staring at her.

"Go on," he said finally.

"That's all there is," Ruby said. "It happened June of the same year, don't you see?"

"The same year as what?" the sheriff said, his face as blank as a sheet of clean paper.

"When I showed up here in Way Down!" Ruby said. "Don't you think that's peculiar?"

The sheriff glanced at Miss Arbutus, then shuffled his feet under his desk and began to play nervously with a pencil.

"Don't you see, she had red curly hair like mine, she was very young, she disappeared without a trace, and I turned up here around the same time."

"But didn't you say she was eaten by a panther?" the sheriff said, obviously bewildered.

"That's what they figured," Ruby said, "but nobody knew for sure. There was never a trace of her found."

The sheriff's face lit up.

"Oh! Oh! I get it!" he cried out. "You're wondering if . . . if . . . I see! Maybe she wadn't eaten up by a panther a'tall!"

Ruby nodded.

"And maybe she was you?"

Ruby nodded again.

The sheriff looked at Miss Arbutus and smiled as if seeking her approval for his cleverness. Miss Arbutus stared out the window at Busy Street and patted Rita's bare leg.

"But how would she get here?" the sheriff said to Ruby. "A little girl like that in the dark. Yonder Mountain is a good piece from here."

Ruby shrugged. "How far is it?"

"A good piece," the sheriff repeated. "And you said her name was Jolene. But your name is Ruby."

"We don't really know my name, do we?" Ruby said. "I mean . . . I was only a toddler. I couldn't talk plain."

The sheriff was trying to comprehend that statement, and it seemed that he was not having much luck.

"We don't have all the answers, Sheriff." Miss Arbutus spoke up. "That's why we came to you. We thought you might want to investigate."

"I do want to investigate," the sheriff said without enthusiasm. "I mean . . . I reckon I should."

Miss Arbutus kindly tried to help him out. "Maybe you should call the law over there in Virginia and see what you can learn."

"Why, Miss Arbutus, that's a real good idea!" the sheriff said. "No matter what anybody else says, *I've* never thought you were dull-witted!"

The sheriff's words hung in the air like a bad odor, and he bit his lip as if he longed to take them back. But Miss Arbutus retained her calm demeanor.

"All righty!" The sheriff tried to sound cheerful. "Y'all go on home now, and I'll take care of everything."

19

THAT VERY AFTERNOON A DETECTIVE BY THE NAME OF Holland came from Buchanan County, Virginia, to see Ruby at The Roost. He was tall with a pleasant face, and he listened to Ruby's brief story without making a comment. In fact, Ruby thought he must have something else on his mind.

She figured a detective probably got leads every day, and if he followed all of them, he would be like a dog chasing its tail. So this Mr. Holland would probably treat her story as just another dead end. After asking her a few questions, he thanked her politely and left.

And that was that, Ruby thought with relief, and went back to helping Miss Arbutus make corn bread for supper.

Detective Holland, however, was not as uninterested as he seemed. He was, in fact, having trouble keeping his excitement concealed as he listened to Ruby's story. On leaving The Roost, he hurried to the courthouse to report to the sheriff.

"She looks exactly like her mother," he said as he dropped himself in the same wingback chair Miss Arbutus had occupied earlier. "She was Jo Combs from Yonder Mountain—prettiest girl you ever saw. She married Clayton Hurley. We called him Clay. I went to school with both of them."

Sheriff Reynolds was too flabbergasted to respond.

"The missing girl was named Ruby Jolene Hurley," Detective Holland went on. "I would swear on a stack of Bibles she's the same child."

"What . . . what should we do?" asked Sheriff Reynolds.

Holland stood up, walked to the window, and looked out at Busy Street.

"Maybe I'll bring her Uncle Christian over here to see her before we do anything."

"Her uncle?"

"Yeah, her mama's brother, Christian Combs. He lives over there near Yonder Mountain."

"What about her mama? Why not bring her? Or her daddy?"

The detective from Virginia sighed a long, weary sigh. "That's a sad story," he said. "I won't go into it now."

The next day, as Ruby was weeding the garden, Miss Arbutus came out and said to her softly, "Someone is here to see you, Ruby June. Do you want to go comb your hair and wash your face?"

"Do I need to?" Ruby said, wiping her hands on her shorts.

Miss Arbutus touched Ruby's hair with tenderness, and shook her head. "Not really. You look beautiful."

"Who is it?" Ruby asked.

"A man from Yonder Mountain. His name is Christian Combs."

Miss Arbutus led her into the common room, where a paunchy middle-aged man with thin red hair and a face full of large freckles sat on a couch beside Sheriff Reynolds. With straw hat in hand, the man stood up to greet Ruby. Detective Holland, who had been standing by the door watching the pansies dance in the sunshine, turned to face the room again.

When Ruby walked up to Christian Combs and said hello, the man's knees gave way on him, and he sank back onto the couch.

"You feel okay?" Ruby said with concern. "You don't look too good."

"It's her," Christian barely whispered. "I know it's her. It's like looking at Jo when she was a girl."

"That was my first reaction exactly!" Holland agreed. "She's the spittin' image of her mama."

"My mama?" Ruby squeaked.

"Yeah, honey," Holland said. "If you're who I think you are, your mama was this man's sister. She was Jo Combs, and your daddy was Clay Hurley, a friend of mine. Your name is Ruby Jolene Hurley."

Ruby could not speak. She turned to look at Miss Arbutus, who was still standing quietly in the doorway that led into the dining room, one hand in her apron pocket.

Miss Arbutus gave Ruby a sad, sweet smile, then faced the detective and said, "You have to have some proof."

"Well, ma'am," Holland said to her, "I think all the evidence we have so far—when she showed up here, her apparent age, her name, her appearance—all that would be about enough to convince anybody."

"You have to have something else."

"Such as?" Holland said.

"Information about what she was wearing that night."

"She was in a homemade petticoat," the sheriff blurted out. "Everybody saw that."

"Something no one knows except me."

Everybody stared at Miss Arbutus.

"And her mother. She would know," Miss Arbutus added.

"Her mother is dead," Christian Combs said bluntly.

"Dead?" Ruby's voice failed her.

"Yes, and your father, too," he said more gently. "They died before you . . . before you got lost."

Ruby could not absorb it all. She felt no pain, no grief for those people who had died. She did not know them. She was numb.

"Then who was that girl staying with?" Ruby asked.

"What girl?" Christian Combs said.

"That little Ruby Jolene Hurley."

"With my mother, Goldie Combs, her grandma . . . *your* grandma." Then he turned to Miss Arbutus. "Are you talking about a pair of little girl's blue cotton step-ins with *R-U-B-Y* embroidered in red across the bottom?"

Miss Arbutus's face paled, and she sank into a nearby chair, her hand still in her apron pocket.

"My mother had to describe to the law what the baby was wearing," Christian said. "That's how she hung on to the memory. It was a habit of Jo's—to embroider Ruby's name on her things. When she was a girl herself, she embroidered her own name on her clothes."

Slowly Miss Arbutus pulled her hand from her pocket and produced an item. Lovingly she spread it across her knee. It was a toddler's pair of underpants, blue in color, with *R-U-B-Y* prominently displayed in red across the bottom.

Ruby walked over and stood beside Miss Arbutus, gazing at the underpants. "I was wearing those?"

Miss Arbutus looked up into Ruby's eyes, so clear, so blue, so trusting. "Yes, nobody ever saw them but me and perhaps Mrs. Doctor," she whispered. "I put them away that same day and brought them out again only now."

Ruby turned to the detective. "But how did I get here?" she said earnestly, her face clouded with confusion. "How far away is Yonder Mountain?"

"Sixty miles," Detective Holland said. "And that's the question all right. How did you get here?"

20

In the following days Ruby and Miss Arbutus traveled with Sheriff Reynolds to Virginia, where they appeared before a judge, along with Detective Holland and Christian Combs. There Ruby's fate was decided, at least temporarily.

"She needs to ease herself gradually into this new situation," the judge said kindly. "I suggest she be taken to Yonder Mountain for a visit before she is permanently removed from the only home she has ever known."

Christian Combs stood up. "And after that, what?"

"Then she needs to come back and talk to me."

Christian Combs continued. "Your honor, as you know, the girl's grandmother, Goldie Combs of Yonder Mountain, was not well enough to appear here today, but she has instructed me to say that she is the girl's legal guardian and she wants her returned unconditionally."

"I know that, Mr. Combs," the judge snapped. "But wouldn't you agree this is a peculiar case? I don't want to make a hasty decision with the child's life."

Christian Combs sat down without saying more.

"Now do as I say. Take her to Yonder Mountain for a visit."

Then the judge turned to Detective Holland and instructed him to continue his investigation into Ruby's disappearance.

"I would like to know what happened to this girl that night on the mountain."

"So would I," Holland said.

Now it was the first day of summer once again, the day Ruby and Miss Arbutus had always celebrated as Ruby's birthday because it was the day she had showed up at the courthouse. But on this birthday Ruby found herself sitting in the front seat of Christian Combs's green DeSoto, heading out of Way Down Deep onto the highway toward Yonder Mountain. She could see the road winding between the hills toward Virginia. The air was heavy and the sky looked like rain.

"You can call me Uncle Chris," Christian Combs said. "I guess you want to hear about Jo and Clay—your mama and daddy."

Ruby felt like her heart was too battered and bruised to go on beating. Hearing about Jo and Clay would only damage it further. She said nothing, but studied her uncle's face.

This man had known her mama as a little girl and as a teenager and as a grownup married woman, too. And he had known her father. She should want to know about that. But still her mind would not go there. It kept going back to the place she had left behind.

"My sister and Clay met at the county high school and courted for about two years before they ran away and eloped on an Easter weekend," Uncle Chris began.

"Why did they run away?"

"Because Mama thought they were too young to marry."

"How old were they?"

"Only seventeen. Clay seemed older because he had kinda raised himself, you see. He grew up in an orphanage and never knew who his people were."

Uncle Chris glanced over at Ruby. She was reading the Burma-Shave signs that appeared at intervals by the roadside.

Don't take

    A curve at

        Sixty per

            We hate to lose

                A customer

                    ****BURMA-SHAVE****

But Ruby was also thinking very hard. And she kept coming back to one question: How could she possibly take on another life and toss away the past like a pair of worn-out shoes?

"They set up housekeeping in a shack down at the foot of the mountain," Uncle Chris went on. "Clay started working in the coal mines, and Jo didn't like that a bit because it was bad for his lungs. He had asthma. She kept after him to find something else, and I'll have to say, he did try, but there was nothing else to be found. Then you came along, and—"

"When is my birthday?" Ruby interrupted him.

Uncle Chris scratched his head. "You know, I'm not real sure. I'm not good at remembering dates. But your grandma will know. She remembers stuff like that."

"Well, how old am I?"

Her uncle scratched his head again. "Twelve, thirteen maybe. I'm not sure, Ruby Jo."

"Was that what everybody called me—Ruby Jo?"

"No, that's the name your folks gave you, but it seemed like everybody had a different name for you. Your mama and daddy just called you Ruby, but after they died, your grandma, well, she didn't like that name, Ruby, so she started calling you Jolene. That was your mama's whole name, you know."

There was silence for a moment in the car. Ruby was thinking that she liked Ruby Jo better than just Ruby or just Jolene. Ruby Jo had something of her mother, and was also not so different from Ruby June.

"Yeah, your grandma wouldn't call you anything but Jolene," Uncle Chris said. "And after you went to live with her, she insisted that everybody else call you Jolene, too."

Uncle Chris lit a cigarette and blew the smoke out the window. Ruby's mind went back to Miss Arbutus.

"We'll celebrate your birthday when you find out the real date," Miss Arbutus had said.

"That sounds good," Ruby said as she and Miss Arbutus packed a few clothes and personal belongings in her suitcase. "And I don't want to say goodbye to anybody before I leave!"

"I understand," Miss Arbutus said softly. "You don't need their sadness dragging you down."

"That's exactly right!" Ruby said. She sat on the suitcase and snapped it shut. "You can tell them whatever you want, but make sure they understand I am coming back soon. I know for sure I am coming home for Kids' Day, and even before then if possible."

"If these people are not good to you, you don't have to stay that long!" Miss Arbutus told her. "Just let me know and I will send somebody for you."

"I won't stay any longer than I have to," Ruby said, not even considering the possibility that she might like her kin. "Surely they will not want me to stay if I'm unhappy there."

Neither she nor Miss Arbutus had mentioned that perhaps Ruby would not have a choice about the matter. The old grandmother had the law on her side.

"Ruby's grandma has mourned for her all these years," Uncle Chris had told the judge. "She lost our dad when Jo was a baby. Then she lost Jo and Ruby within a few months of each other. All that grief aged her before her time."

Rain started in small splatters against the windshield. Uncle Chris threw his cigarette butt out and rolled the window up. In the distance Ruby could see patches of clouds quivering in the hollows.

21

"How do you think I got from Yonder Mountain to Way Down, Uncle Chris?"

"I have no idea, but it stands to reason that somebody took you."

"I don't remember anything about it now, but they say I told everybody I had come on a horse."

"I heard that from the sheriff. But it don't seem likely, does it? I can't think of a soul who had a riding horse at that time, and besides, I don't think a horse could travel that far in one night."

"A car could do it easy," Ruby said. "It must have been a car."

"It *had* to be a car," her uncle said. "But we were all poor folks up on that mountain. We had no cars. To this day, you can't even drive a car up there. Somebody who wanted to take you would have to walk up the mountain in the middle of the night, steal you off the porch and haul you down the mountain without making a sound, put you in his car, and then drive you to West Virginia and dump you out. I reckon it could be done, but who would do that? And why? It don't make a bit of sense to me. Not a bit."

"Who else was in the house that night?" Ruby asked.

"Your grandma, me and my wife, and our six kids."

"So that's who the other kids were on the porch? Your kids? How old were they?"

"They had some size to them. I was lots older than Jo, you know, so I already had my family half raised before she got started. That night y'all slept on the porch together was ten years ago, and my three oldest ones, all girls, are married now, two of them with kids of their own. The three boys are still at home with me and the wife. They are Jeff, Sam, and Sidney, all teenagers."

"And who lives with my grandma now?" Ruby asked.

"Nobody. My wife and me took the kids and moved out a few years ago."

"Where do y'all live?" Ruby asked.

"Down at the mouth of the holler at the foot of Yonder Mountain. Where you're going is way up to the top of the mountain."

"How on earth does a little old lady live up there on the top of a mountain all by herself? She must be afraid!"

"Afraid of what?" Uncle Chris bellowed so loud, Ruby was startled. "There ain't nothing on that mountain meaner than she is!"

And he laughed like he had told a very funny joke. Ruby watched him with puzzled eyes. This was his mother he was talking about.

"What I mean is—" Uncle Chris abruptly changed his

tune and took on a serious face. "I mean she's a brave woman, always has been, not afraid of anything."

They both lapsed into silence. The WELCOME TO VIRGINIA sign rose up before them. Ruby stared at it until they had passed. Then she turned around and looked behind until it faded away. The mountains were a hazy blue in the pouring rain.

"Tell me how my mama and daddy died," Ruby said at last.

"It was during the war." Christian began his story. "Clay missed the draft because of his asthma. Word came to the hills from the shipyards in Norfolk, Virginia, that any able-bodied man who was not in the war and wanted work would find it there in Norfolk. I reckon they couldn't keep up with the wartime demand.

"Clay and Jo jumped at the chance to leave the coal mines behind. By this time you had come along, and I reckon they thought you would have a better future out there. So they packed up their belongings and took the train out to Norfolk with only a few dollars in their pockets.

"We figured they'd be back hungry and broke in a matter of days. But we were wrong. Clay found a good job, and they rented a pretty decent apartment, a nicer place than they had here anyhow, and they stayed. And they bought themselves an old rattletrap—a Ford, I think it was.

"I don't recollect exactly when they went or how long they were there, but sometime in February of 1944 we got a telegram from the police in Norfolk that Jo and Clay both had been killed. The roads were slick with snow and ice, and the tires on that old car were plumb bald. They had skidded into a moving train."

Uncle Chris stopped there. Ruby closed her eyes and pictured that long-ago February.

Snow. Lots of snow. Her memory of being rocked could have come from that same day her parents were killed! Suddenly she also remembered icicles hanging from the gutters. Yes, there was a bitter cold outside, while warm arms cradled her inside. A deep sadness came over her.

"Where was I?" she said. "Why wasn't I in the car, too?"

"As I understand it, your mama went to pick your daddy up after his shift ended. It was close to midnight, and she didn't want to take you out in the weather. So she left you with an old woman who lived in the next apartment.

"I didn't have a car myself, but I borrowed one and drove out to Norfolk to get you and your family's stuff. The old woman was real attached to the three of you, but I've forgot her name now. Still, I do remember what she told me were the last words your mama said to you.

"Jo was all bundled up in her heavy clothes, and she bent over and kissed you and said, 'Ruby, you wait right here for me. I'll be back soon.' "

Woo-bee is right here waiting for you.

"Then you came to live up on the mountain with your

grandma, and me and my wife and our six kids, for the next four months, until you vanished in the night."

The rain had stopped, and a sign by the road read,

YONDER MOUNTAIN ↑

The arrow pointed up a gravel road that snaked through the hollow between the hills. Uncle Chris turned the DeSoto onto the road.

"That's where I live," he said, pointing to a white frame house beside a small country store that stood in the crook of the intersection. The store had Chesterfield cigarette ads tacked all over the outside.

He drove right on by.

"Me and the wife bought the store a few years back. She's looking after it today, and the boys are at football camp."

Ruby wondered why her uncle hadn't stopped and introduced her to his wife, but she didn't ask.

"What's your wife's name?"

"Maxine. You can call her Aunt Max."

Going up the holler, they drove by only two houses, which were spaced far apart. Then her uncle pulled the car over to one side, where a path curled up the mountain and vanished into the trees.

"This is the path to your grandma's house," Uncle Chris said as he jerked the hand brake into place and climbed out of the car.

He unlocked the trunk and removed Ruby's suitcase.

Ruby opened her door, placed her feet on the ground, and studied the path. It was even steeper than the one leading to Way Up That-a-Way. Her uncle walked ahead of her, carrying the luggage.

The trees were dripping from the recent rain, and there was mud on the path. Ruby picked her way carefully so she wouldn't mess up the new white moccasins that Miss Arbutus had given to her before she left The Roost.

"They are either an early or a late birthday present," Miss Arbutus had said. "Just wear them back to me soon."

The sun began to speckle the ground through the trees. Ruby breathed in deeply, as she had always loved the smell of the earth after a summer rain.

They had not gone far when Uncle Chris began wheezing with the effort of climbing the hill. He stopped to rest and leaned against a tree.

"I can carry the suitcase," Ruby offered.

"Oh, no, I've got it."

They repeated the same ritual several times. Ruby was not as tuckered as her uncle was, and finally he did hand the suitcase to her.

He mopped his brow with a handkerchief. "It's not much farther."

22

WHEN THEY REACHED THE TOP OF THE MOUNTAIN, RUBY saw a wood frame house ahead at the edge of the woods. It was not made of polished logs like Granny Butler's house but of rough boards, weathered gray. There was no nice slate walkway, nor flowers or green grass, only a plain dirt yard with a few chickens scratching about.

The porch was as long as the house, and wide, certainly roomy enough for seven children to bed down on a hot night. So this was where it had happened, Ruby thought. Then why did none of this look familiar to her? Why did she get no feeling, no sense of having been here before?

Uncle Chris stepped up onto the porch and opened the door for Ruby. She went inside. The main room was a kitchen and living room—dark, lifeless, colorless, bare. Ruby set her suitcase down on the floor as her uncle went into a room that appeared to be a bedroom.

"Did you bring the girl?" someone said.

Uncle Chris motioned Ruby to come into the room.

Lying in the bed, with a ratty sheet tucked under her chin, was a rather large-boned unkempt woman with wiry gray hair. A few wrinkles lined her eyes and mouth, but she did not seem as ancient as Ruby had imagined.

Standing before her grandmother, Ruby was slightly ashamed that she felt no affection for the woman in the bed, and hoped she would not be asked to kiss her cheek. She was not.

The pale blue eyes studied Ruby for a long moment before the old woman spoke.

"You can thank your Grandpa Combs for the hair. You favor him, just like your mama did."

Ruby did not know what to say.

"Can you cook?" the old woman asked.

Ruby nodded, thinking what a strange question it was to be asking a grandchild you had not seen in ten years.

"Who learned you to cook?"

"I learned by helping Miss Arbutus," Ruby said, not knowing whether she should explain who Miss Arbutus was. How much would Uncle Chris have told his mother?

"The boardinghouse woman." Uncle Chris spoke up.

Grandma Combs didn't even glance at him. She kept her attention on Ruby.

"Jolene, you sound like your mama, and you look like her, too."

"I prefer to be called Ruby Jo," Ruby said.

The old lady glared at her.

"I mean if it's okay with you," Ruby added.

Uncle Chris cleared his throat nervously and said,

"Well, I gotta be going. Y'all get acquainted, and I'll come back tomorrow to see how you're doing."

Grandma Combs turned to him then and roared, "Liar! You won't come back until delivery day!"

Ruby was alarmed. When was delivery day? It sounded about as far off as Judgment Day.

"Oh, n-no," he stammered. "I'll be b-back tomorrow to see if Rub—Jolene needs anything. Then I'll bring up your groceries and mail as usual on Saturday."

"Huh!" Grandma Combs snorted.

But Uncle Chris was gone.

"Well, don't just stand there, Jolene!" Ruby's grandma barked at her. "Pull up a chair and tell me about yourself."

Ruby glanced around. There were two straight-back kitchen chairs against the wall. She pulled one of them to her grandma's bedside and sat down.

"Well, I—" Ruby began.

"Did they tell you I'm a sick woman?" her grandma interrupted.

"Yes. What's wrong with you?"

"What do you mean, what's wrong with me? I'm sick! That's what's wrong with me."

"I know, but I mean sick with what? Do you have a heart condition or a disease . . . or something?"

"I'm sick of living, that's what!" the old woman declared. "I'm old! I'm old and sick of living."

"You don't look old. Your hair is gray, but your face is not wrinkled up too bad."

"Is that right? Well, I wouldn't know. I ain't seen a

looking glass since your mama broke it the year she was fourteen!"

"How old are you, anyhow?" Ruby asked.

Her grandma glared at her again.

Ruby stared at her hands and muttered, "Sorry."

"I don't rightly know how old I am," Grandma Combs said. "I've lost track of time. I know I was born in 1894. Can you cipher?"

"Yes, ma'am."

Ruby did a quick mental calculation. "You're only sixty years old, Grandma."

Her grandma seemed surprised. "Are you sure? You did that awful fast. What year is it?"

"It's 1954. Don't you have a calendar?"

"What for? One year's like another up here on the mountain."

"Do you know when my birthday is?"

"Yeah, it's the same as mine, October 2."

Ruby felt a small thrill. She had a real birthday.

"So what year was I born?" she asked.

"Nineteen forty-one," her grandma said. "And that makes you how old?"

"I'll be thirteen," Ruby said. "It's nice that we have the same birthday."

"When your mama told me that *you* were my birthday present the year you were born, I told her not to give me no more presents, thank you very much. Last thing in the world she needed was a baby. And then I'm the one left holding the bag when . . . she . . ."

Grandma Combs didn't finish her sentence, but lay staring into one corner of the room, as if she saw ghostly memories lurking there in the shadows.

"Jolene, how did you get to West Virginia?"

"I don't know. I don't remember."

"Are you lying to me?"

Ruby was insulted. "I don't lie," she said.

"Huh!" her grandma snorted. "I never saw a Combs that didn't lie."

"I don't remember anything. If I did, I would tell you."

"It's had me puzzled these ten years," Grandma said. "We woke up that morning and found you gone, and all the young'uns said they didn't hear or see a thing in the night. Folks on the other side of the mountain said they heard a panther screaming in the dark, but we didn't hear it over here."

"I'm just as puzzled as you are," Ruby said.

"And then you turn up ten years later sixty miles away."

"Maybe the panther took me to West Virginia," Ruby said, trying to get a smile out of her grandma.

But Grandma turned her head away from Ruby and closed her eyes. Ruby sat perfectly still for what seemed like a long time. She didn't dare breathe, because she hoped Grandma had gone to sleep. But no such luck. The woman opened her eyes.

"Go on, fix us a bite to eat!"

Ruby said, "Beg your pardon?" because Miss Arbutus had taught her not to say "Huh?"

But Grandma mocked her attempt at politeness. "Beg your pardon! Beg your pardon!" she parroted.

Ruby was stunned. Never before had a grownup person made fun of her like this.

"I don't like such proud talking!" Grandma hissed. "Now go fix me something to eat!"

Without another word, Ruby got up and went into the main room. She pushed her suitcase against the wall, then peeped into one of the kitchen cabinets. The first shelf held cans of vegetables, and above it were macaroni, cornmeal, oatmeal, and brown sugar.

She entered a small room behind the kitchen, which served as a combination pantry and laundry room. There she found a couple of salt-cured hams hanging from nails, also potatoes, onions, apples, and more.

Ruby almost missed the door that apparently led to the outside from this small room. On finding it, she eased it open and looked out onto a back porch where the woods had encroached. Vines curled around the railing, and weeds pushed their way up through the cracks between the floor slats. She glanced into the darkness of the forest, closed the door quickly, and latched it.

She would start with the cornmeal, mix it with eggs and milk, and have corn bread. Then she would slice some ham and fry it with potatoes and onions. Add to that spring lettuce and baby cucumbers, and her first meal for Grandma was soon in progress.

23

WHEN SUPPER WAS READY ALMOST AN HOUR LATER, RUBY tiptoed to the bedroom door and timidly called, "It's on the table, Grandma."

"It's not doing me any good on the table, now, is it? Bring it to me, child! Bring it in here."

Again Ruby was astonished. So she was expected to serve her grandma in bed? But Miss Arbutus had taught Ruby to obey her elders, so she filled up a plate and carried it to the bedroom.

"Do you want a glass of water to drink?" she asked. "Or some milk?"

"Ain't there a bottle of pop somewhere?" Grandma said, sitting up on the side of the bed and pulling a small table close to her.

Ruby set the plate down and returned to the kitchen for pop. When she brought it back, Grandma was eating heartily. It seemed her illness had not spoiled her appetite. She didn't look up from her plate, or speak, so Ruby went into the kitchen to feed herself.

The sun was going down as she sat at the small wooden table beside the kitchen window. She looked out at the mountaintop stretching away toward the sky. How peculiar it seemed to be here, high above the hollers and streams with the sky right on top of you. It was a pretty place, but so far away from everybody. So isolated it felt like the jumping-off place at the edge of the world.

She couldn't help thinking it was the first time in her life that she had eaten a meal all by herself. What were they eating for supper at The Roost? What was the topic of conversation? Probably poor Ruby June. She had no appetite for the food, but she sighed and forced herself to eat. It was for sure she was going to need her strength.

After cleaning up the kitchen, she went back into her grandma's bedroom. "Where should I sleep?"

"Anywhere you want. There's two doors in there off the living room. One's the bathroom, and one's a bedroom. You can move in there—that is, if it's good enough for you after living in that highfalutin boardinghouse!"

Ruby didn't respond. She was relieved to know there was a bathroom. She had heard stories of people living in the hills who had nothing but outdoor toilets.

"There's two more bedrooms upstairs," Grandma added. "But it's hot up there."

"Oh, I didn't realize there were two floors," Ruby said. "You can't tell from the outside."

"It's just the attic," Grandma explained. "When your mama was born, your grandpa made two bedrooms out of it. The eaves are low, but I reckon it'll do for a short person."

"How do you get up there?" Ruby asked.

"A trapdoor in the ceiling of the pantry."

Ruby pulled her suitcase into the downstairs bedroom, and turned on the lamp beside the bed. It was a small room, but cozy. The bedspread was ruffled and pink, with curtains to match.

Though all the other walls in the house were bare, somebody had used wallpaper samples to decorate this room, and the effect was strangely sweet. There were flowers here and ribbons there, horses and dogs in open fields, and willow trees beside still waters, also brightly colored parasols flying into an endless blue sky.

Ruby was unpacking and placing her belongings in a bureau beside the window when she was startled by urgent yelling from her grandma.

"Jolene! Jolene! Come here!"

Ruby rushed to her grandma's side.

"What is it?" she inquired breathlessly as she entered the room.

"Open that window for me!" Grandma commanded.

Ruby felt a twinge of irritation. "I thought something was wrong," she said.

"There *is* something wrong! I'm hot. It's stuffy in here. It's the first night of summer, you know!"

Of course she knew it was the first night of summer. "How do you know that without a calendar?" she asked her grandma as she opened the window.

"By the moon! That's how! I may not keep up with the years, but I can read the moon's phases and count days. I'm not stupid!"

Ruby hesitated before going back to her room. Did her grandma remember that *it* had happened on the first night of summer? But no, she decided, she would not bring up the subject again.

She went to her room and sat down on the bed. How strange it was to be returning to this place ten years to the day after disappearing from it! She thought of the dark woods taking over the back porch, and shivered. Suppose . . . just suppose that whatever occurred on that fateful night repeated itself tonight?

The bathroom was much smaller than the one she had shared with Miss Arbutus at The Roost. And it did not have those special touches, like candles and sweet-smelling soap. It was, in fact, dirty, and Ruby wondered how long her grandma had been sick to let the place go like this.

She took a hasty bath and returned to her room, put on her thin summer nightgown, and turned down the sheets. They did not smell fresh like the ones at The Roost. Probably nobody had used this room for a long time. But never mind, she would wash the sheets tomorrow.

She placed her stationery on the nightstand and climbed into the small bed. She wrote a letter to Miss Arbutus before turning out her lamp.

Deep in the night she was dreaming of being a little girl again and playing May I? in the school yard.

"Take a giant step off the mountaintop!"

"May I?"

"Yes, you may."

As Ruby was stepping off the edge of the world, she woke up with a start. She could not see a speck of light anywhere. She could hear Grandma Combs snoring and the cries of various night creatures, but nothing more.

She settled back into her pillow and thought of the moment she had said goodbye to Miss Arbutus.

"See you soon!" Ruby had called with more cheeriness than she felt.

Then she had climbed into Uncle Chris's car to begin her journey, and Miss Arbutus had gone quickly into the house.

She had been aware of Peter, Cedar, Bird, and Rita standing on the sidewalk watching her leave, but she pretended not to see them. Then Peter had walked up to the open car window, and she could not avoid him.

"Bird is awful glad you were not eaten by a panther," he said. "And so am I."

Ruby forced herself to smile. "See you on Kids' Day, Peter, if not before. Bye for now!" And she had deliberately turned away from him to speak to Uncle Chris. "Okay, let's go."

"That's the Reeder family, right?" Uncle Chris inquired.

Ruby nodded.

"The old man used to come around to plow for us. I

think I know Bob, too, but I've not seen the kids before. Good-looking young'uns, ain't they?"

Ruby had not responded.

"They lived on the other side of the mountain from us, so we didn't see much of them."

Now, all alone in her little room on the mountain, Ruby recalled the way Peter had spoken so sweetly to her, how nice his hair had looked after a good cut at Mr. Bevins's barbershop, how Cedar had scowled at her.

She smiled to herself, thinking he was probably doing some classic cussing in his head.

And poor little Rita had simply stood there twisting her dirty dress tail into a wad.

Ruby drifted into troubled dreams again. Beyond the back porch she was struggling through the woods. Dark and deep and tangled woods, with gnarled trees. And full of eyes. Green eyes. But she could not hesitate, for she was following a sound. She had to find it. Had to. It was far and then near. Loud and then faint. It was a small child weeping as if her heart would break.

"Mommie! Mommie!"

24

"JOLENE! JOLENE! GET UP!"

It was Goldie Combs pounding on Ruby's door, wrenching her from a deep sleep very early next morning. She leapt from bed and flung open the door.

"What is it? What's wrong?"

The large woman stood there in a nightgown, pushing uncombed hair from her face.

"I'm hungry," she said peevishly. "I want biscuits for breakfast."

Ruby was afraid she could not hide her irritation, so she stumbled past the woman quickly and went to the bathroom to wash the sleep from her face.

Thus began her second day on the mountain. While Ruby was cleaning up the kitchen after breakfast, her grandma came in with a towel and said she felt well enough to take a bath this morning. Ruby was glad to hear it.

Ruby waited until her grandma was finished bathing

before she gathered all the dirty laundry. The washing machine was the wringer type very much like the one Miss Arbutus used. Ruby started a load of linens, then went out to feed the chickens from a bag of dried corn. She was scrubbing the crud from the bathroom when the old woman yelled again.

"Jolene! Come here! Jolene!"

Ruby groaned and bit her lip, but this time she walked calmly to her grandma's room.

At that very moment in Way Down Deep, old Mrs. Rife was walking into the laundry room at The Roost. Miss Arbutus was deep in thought as she pushed her own linens through the wringer, and was startled to hear a voice behind her.

"I called her a mangy stray one time."

Miss Arbutus turned to face Mrs. Rife. She nodded at her and stood waiting for her to say more.

"The girl," Mrs. Rife explained. "Ruby June. I called her a mangy stray and I threw rocks at her."

Still Miss Arbutus said nothing.

"So I came by to say I'm sorry."

Miss Arbutus gave her a slight smile.

"I'm sorry and I won't do it again. I promised God. I made a deal with him. I promised him I would not throw rocks at anybody ever again, if he would let Ruby June come back to us."

At that, Miss Arbutus walked to the old woman and placed a hand on her arm. Then they had a cup of tea together.

"I'm afraid I've been a bad girl, but I can't seem to help myself." Mrs. Rife tried to explain her behavior as she sipped her tea. "I throw rocks at all the boys and girls—tall ones and short ones, black and white, skinny and fat, clever and stupid . . ." She paused and took a breath. "So you'll have to admit I haven't been a bit prejudiced. I hate them all equally."

Together she and Miss Arbutus had a good laugh, following the philosophy that laughter is the best medicine.

Later in the afternoon, Miss Arbutus did an unusual thing—not as unusual as traveling all the way to another state to appear before a judge—but unusual enough to cause curious neighbors to pull aside their curtains and watch her.

She walked to the house where the Reeders lived, and knocked on the frame of the screen door. Peter answered the knock.

"Oh, hey, Miss Arbutus. Come in!" he said, obviously surprised to see her.

Cedar walked up beside Peter.

"I came to borrow Rita," Miss Arbutus said.

"Say what?" Cedar said, wrinkling up his forehead.

"I want to borrow Rita for a while."

The boys just looked at her.

"I need somebody to dote on," Miss Arbutus explained.

The curious eyes of the neighbors watched Miss Arbutus walk back to The Roost, leading the little girl by the hand, one as silent as the other.

Goldie Combs was right. Uncle Chris did not come to see if Ruby needed anything that day, as he had said he would. After supper she told Ruby to drop everything and come in and sit down.

"Now talk to me," she ordered. "And don't use big words. I don't like big words."

"Well, I—"

"You're sleeping in your mama's room," Grandma Combs interrupted. "She's the one put all that stuff on the wall."

"You mean the wallpaper samples?"

"Yeah, and the writing on the wallpaper."

Ruby was surprised. "I didn't see any writing."

"Well, you have to look close and squint. She wrote real tiny. Her teachers always grumbled about that."

Ruby was eager to see what her mother had written, but she would wait until she was excused.

Still, she had to ask, "What did she have to say?"

"How should I know?" Grandma was cross again. "Or even care? She always had too *much* to say. That was her problem. Besides, I can't see anything that little. Maybe you can read it."

"Don't you have reading glasses?" Ruby asked. She knew quite a lot about reading glasses, as Miss Arbutus, Mrs. Thornton Elkins, Mr. Crawford, and practically everybody over forty who came to The Roost had to wear them.

"Reading glasses! Who do you think I am, the Queen of England? We don't have reading glasses up here on this mountain."

Ruby didn't believe that was true. Glasses were not some newfangled gadget. And she knew they were not very expensive.

"I will ask Miss Arbutus to send you a pair, if you like," she offered.

Grandma narrowed her eyes and looked at Ruby with distrust. "For how much!"

"Miss Arbutus would be glad to buy you a pair of glasses," Ruby said with confidence. "Mr. Doctor sells them in his waiting room. He will give her a discount."

"Who's Mr. Doctor?"

"He's the town doctor in Way Down, and he takes care of everybody's health, including their eyes, but not their teeth. His wife is Mrs. Doctor, the dentist. Mrs. Doctor does a good business, cleaning and filling and pulling teeth.

"Their last name is Justus, but you can see how that would get confusing, to have two Dr. Justuses, so—"

"I get it, I get it," the old lady mumbled.

"Anyhow, the doctors are not rich, by any means, because it is the general belief of Way Down people that you only get sick when you're unhappy. So they stay as happy as possible. Most of Mr. Doctor's business is delivering babies, giving shots, and stuff like that.

"He could make lots more money if he moved to a sad town, but the people in Way Down want to keep him. So when the word gets around that Mr. Doctor's side of the waiting room is empty, the people put their heads together and plan appointments for routine checkups."

Grandma pretended not to be interested in the doctors. She frowned as she picked aimlessly at her sheets, then scowled, and fluffed up her pillow. But somehow Ruby knew that she had finally said something Grandma wanted to hear, and that she was listening to every word. So Ruby went on and on, telling her as many stories as she could recall about Mr. and Mrs. Doctor.

When Grandma let her go, Ruby cleaned up the kitchen before going to her room to search the wallpaper for her mother's writing.

She found it first among the parasols, where the blue sky allowed wide clean spaces for writing. Ruby was immediately enchanted, for the young Jo Combs had written notes to her dead father!

Dear Daddy, I wish you were here. We have a new calf. Her name is Ruby. That is my favorite name. You would love her. She has a star on her forehead. Love, Jo

Dear Daddy, The kitten died. And I cried. I thought if you were here you would pet me and tell me don't cry. Love, Jo

Dear Daddy, Chris and Max are married and gone. I am all alone with Mama, and there is no gladness left in her. Love, Jo

Ruby was thoughtful as she dressed for bed. Here was something to occupy her mind. There was enough writing on the walls to last for days, and she would savor it.

25

WHEN UNCLE CHRIS CAME ON SATURDAY, HIS ARMS loaded down with grocery bags, his mother was in the bathroom, taking a bath. Ruby held the door for her uncle.

"This ain't all of it," Uncle Chris said. "The boys have the rest."

"The boys?"

"Yeah, my boys are out there around the corner of the house. They won't come in."

"Why not?"

Uncle Chris set the groceries on the table, then turned to Ruby and shrugged. "I don't know."

She went out with her uncle. Two of the boys had already propped their bags against the house and headed back down the path. But one of them had stayed behind. When Ruby rounded the corner of the house, he was standing there chewing on a blade of grass.

"Hey, cousin!" he said, grinning. "I'm Sidney."

"I'm Ruby," Ruby said, and held out her hand to Sidney. "And I'm awfully glad to meet you."

Sidney laughed out loud. "I bet you are! By this time, you'd be glad to meet the devil his own self!"

"Now, Sidney, don't you be acting smart!" Uncle Chris scolded his youngest son.

Then Uncle Chris picked up the bags from the ground and carried them inside. Ruby lingered on with Sidney.

"What do you mean?" she asked him.

"I mean you must be going crazy with nobody around but Grandma."

"It does get lonely," Ruby confessed.

"Do you have time to get lonely?" Sidney asked. "Don't she keep you jumping at her command?"

"Well . . ." Ruby started to admit it was true, but thought better of it.

"Yeah, they sure pulled a fast one on you," Sidney said with a chuckle.

Ruby found his laughter irritating, as if she were slow-witted, and he was making fun.

"What do you mean?"

"I mean they stuck you up here with the old battleax without telling you how hateful she is, and how hard she is to please. And you have to take it. You can't get away!"

Ruby was speechless. Uncle Chris came out and picked up the last of the bags.

When his father had gone back inside, Sidney said, "She ran everybody else off long ago. Daddy only comes up here 'cause he has to. She helped him buy the store, and he owes her, but he's scared to death of her. Nobody can stand her."

"So that's why you stayed out here in the heat?"

"Yeah, and I wouldn't go in there for water if I was on fire. The minute she sees me, she goes into one of her tirades." Sidney paused. "But hey, maybe you get along with the old girl, huh?"

His eyes twinkled.

Ruby said nothing. For a moment she had the dreadful feeling that she might cry. But she swallowed hard. She would not let her cousin make her cry.

"She needs a lot of help," Ruby said.

"Yeah, Mama used to come up here and do for her, but she couldn't please her. Daddy has hired about a dozen different people to take care of her, but she runs them off. So when Mama and Daddy heard about you, I could see the wheels turning in their heads. 'Yeah!' they were thinking. 'Slave labor!' "

Ruby felt her face go red with anger.

"Why didn't your brothers hang around to meet me?" she said, trying to stay calm.

Sidney laughed. "Oh, them? They're just like Mama. She didn't want to meet you either. She's afraid she may like you, and then she'd feel guilty about sending the lamb to the slaughter."

Ruby couldn't hold back any longer. "Such thoughtful relatives!" she said sarcastically. "Maybe it was an angel of mercy who took me away from here!"

Sidney smirked. Ruby turned on her heel and

stomped away from him. In the kitchen Uncle Chris was storing the perishables in the refrigerator. Ruby began to unload the other bags.

"Doesn't Grandma have to take some kind of medicine?" she asked him. "You didn't bring any, and I haven't seen any around."

"Medicine?" Uncle Chris said. "For what?"

"For whatever ails her."

"Oh, that." Uncle Chris dismissed her question and pointed to the mail on the table. "Letter came for you."

Ruby picked up the envelope and read the return address. It was from Miss Arbutus.

"I have written some letters, too," she said to her uncle. "Will you mail them for me?"

"Sure thing!"

When Ruby brought the letters to Uncle Chris, he said, "I gotta go now. Tell Mama we didn't have any of those pickled pig's feet she likes so much. But I'll bring her some next week."

"You don't want to see her today?" Ruby asked.

"I'm in a bit of a hurry."

"Uncle Chris, how long did the judge say I should stay here before I go back to see him?"

"He didn't say."

Uncle Chris gave her a quick nervous glance and was gone. She watched him go down the path with Sidney. When they were out of sight, Ruby sat and propped her elbows on the table, put her chin in her hands, and let out a long weary sigh. It would be a week before she saw any-body again.

In Way Down, Miss Arbutus and Rita were in the yard petting Jethro.

"He won't climb the woodpile anymore," Miss Arbu-tus was telling Rita. "He just stands here all day long and watches the back door, hoping Ruby June will come out."

Rita turned large sad eyes to Miss Arbutus. Today the child was brightly dressed up in a sunsuit that Ruby had outgrown years ago. It was white with red ladybugs scat-tered all over it.

At that moment somebody opened the screen door, and Jethro lurched in joyful anticipation, but it was only Miss Worly.

"Miss Arbutus," she said. "Do you routinely quench the thirst of the *Viola tricolor hortensis*?"

Miss Arbutus smiled. "Yes, I water the pansies every day."

"Nevertheless, they appear to be in delicate health. I am apprehensive for their continued existence."

"I'm afraid you're right," Miss Arbutus said sadly. "They miss Ruby June so much, they are dying with grief."

26

I GOT A PACKAGE FROM MISS ARBUTUS," RUBY SAID TO Grandma Combs.

Two more Saturdays had passed, and this time her uncle had set the groceries and mail on the porch, not even bothering to come in. Again he had claimed to be in a hurry, and Ruby's cousins could be seen retreating rapidly down the path.

"She sent me some library books, and you some magazines," Ruby said brightly.

Grandma sat up in bed as Ruby handed the magazines to her.

"*Life*," Grandma said almost pleasantly. "I've always enjoyed their pictures."

"Now you can do more than look at the pictures!" Ruby happily announced. "See! Miss Arbutus also sent you a pair of reading glasses!" And Ruby produced the glasses with a flourish.

Without speaking, Grandma put the glasses on.

"Now you can also read what my mama wrote on the

wall!" Ruby said, very pleased with herself that she could do this favor for her grandma.

Grandma grunted.

Ruby lingered, waiting for some kind of reaction from the woman. Finally she had to know.

"Can you read the words in the magazine?"

"Shut up and get out of here!"

Ruby went into her own room, looked at the notes on the wall, and sighed. She knew that Jo Combs had never become hardened to her mother's harshness, nor would she.

In her letters to Miss Arbutus, Ruby had not reported all of her difficulties with Grandma Combs, but she had complained that there was no radio or phonograph or reading material in the house.

Miss Worly had recommended . . . *And Now Miguel* and *Hurry Home, Candy* for Ruby. They were enclosed, along with a Tarzan book and a Trixie Belden mystery, both chosen by Miss Arbutus. Ruby took the four books and placed them on a shelf beside her bed.

While there, she took the time to study once again two special pictures she had tacked onto the wall above the shelf.

The day before, in the ceiling of the room that served as a laundry room and pantry, Ruby had opened the door to the attic and pulled down the steps. Quietly she had explored while her grandma was sleeping. There she had found some of her own baby clothes with *R-U-B-Y* embroidered on them. She had also found pictures of her mother as a child, and a few of Uncle Chris and his kids. But one of the pictures was more special than all the others. On the back, in her mama's small handwriting, she had read:

The Hurleys: Clay, Jo, and Ruby
Norfolk, Virginia, Christmas 1943

Only two months before they were killed! Now Ruby couldn't get enough of staring at it.

There they were—like three kids together. Even in black-and-white her mother sparkled. Ruby guessed that the dress was red in honor of Christmas, and her father wore a dark suit and tie, his eyes and blond hair shining under the photographer's lights. Ruby, in a white dress, bounced on her daddy's knee, and smiled at the camera.

"My mama and daddy were awfully good-looking," she said to herself proudly, perhaps for the hundredth time. "And we were such a happy family. Just look at those smiles!"

The second picture on the wall was one of herself, Peter, and Bird, which Slim had sent to her from the ones he had taken that special Saturday night in Way Down.

Bird was looking at the sky, and Ruby was standing between him and Peter, smiling, totally unaware of the changes about to come. Would she ever get back to that life?

• • •

Later on that evening, at the Roost, Mrs. Thornton Elkins entered the kitchen, where Miss Arbutus was stirring something on the stove. She was running late in preparing supper.

"How much longer do you think it will be?" Mrs. Thornton Elkins asked her.

A less gracious person might have taken offense at being rushed by a charity tenant, but Miss Arbutus, being like she was, apologized.

"I'm sorry," she said in a small voice. "I know you are all hungry. It won't be much longer."

Mrs. Thornton Elkins studied Miss Arbutus's face and thought she detected sorrow there. She could not remember a single time this good lady had been late in preparing a meal. Then an idea popped into her head.

"Could you use some help?" she asked, surprising Miss Arbutus so profoundly that she dropped her stirring spoon on the floor.

Without a word, Mrs. Thornton Elkins bent over for the utensil, wiped up the splatters it had made on the floor, and fetched a clean spoon for Miss Arbutus.

"Perhaps I can do the chores that Ruby June used to do," Mrs. Thornton Elkins said, further surprising Miss Arbutus so that she could not answer.

Being used to Miss Arbutus's silence, Mrs. Thornton Elkins did not realize that the proprietor of The Roost was too taken aback to respond.

"I know Ruby June poured the tea and lemonade,"

Mrs. Thornton Elkins went on, as she timidly opened the refrigerator.

Miss Arbutus finally found her voice. "Ruby Jo," she said.

"Beg your pardon?" said Mrs. Thornton Elkins. Carefully she began to fill glasses with ice.

"She wrote to me that she wants to be called Ruby Jo now."

"Oh, I see. Ruby Jo. That's good. It's nice for her to know who she is at last."

"You can get the salad out of the refrigerator," Miss Arbutus said to her. "And the butter and deviled eggs."

There was silence for a few moments as the two women worked together.

"Thank you, Mrs. Thornton Elkins," Miss Arbutus finally said, almost in a whisper.

"Call me Lucy," Mrs. Thornton Elkins said.

"Beg your pardon?"

"My given name is Lucy."

Miss Arbutus smiled. "Thank you, Lucy."

As Lucy placed napkins on the table, she said softly, "Yes, it's nice to know who you are."

27

SOMETIMES RUBY WENT TO PICK WILDFLOWERS FOR THE kitchen table, just to escape the house. How good it was to be out and away from the demands and insults of her grandma!

Now, toward the end of July, the blackberries were hanging plump and dark on their bushes. So Ruby took a pail to a spot on the mountain that had few trees and lots of sunshine. Here her thoughts were her own without interruption. She looked around at the beauty and loneliness of this place and imagined her mother picking blackberries at this same spot.

Within the past few weeks, she had told her grandma about the Mullins family and their snack bar in a boxcar. She had also talked about the Morgans and their drugstore and old Mrs. Rife, who liked to throw rocks when she was mad. Grandma had liked that story very much.

She had talked about Mr. Farmer, who was so traumatized by the war that he drank liquor to forget; the rhyming Reeders, whom Grandma knew only slightly; the

Fuller triplets and their street preaching; Granny Butler, the albino; Mrs. Bevins and her outlandish outfits; and more.

But she had saved The Roost residents for last.

"I just hope I can hang on here long enough to tell her about them," Ruby said to herself as she placed a handful of berries in the pail.

She looked at her hands, which were stained purple. Miss Arbutus would tell her to wash them with Lava soap, but she had none here. Her fingernails were a disgrace. But Goldie Combs had made fun when Ruby asked her about a nail file.

"Mountain women don't have time to waste on fingernails!" her grandma had snorted. "Just bite 'em off when they get in your way!"

Ruby sighed and figured if she was going to be here much longer, she would have to ask Miss Arbutus to send her manicuring supplies on top of everything else she had asked for—hair bows and bobby pins, a comb, more underwear, more stationery and a fountain pen, a clock, a calendar, a new toothbrush, and she couldn't remember what all else.

After supper Ruby served her grandma a small dish of blackberries with brown sugar and milk.

"They're bitter," Grandma complained.

"I'll fetch you some more sugar."

"No! We all must have our share of bitter berries, Jolene. Don't you know that?"

"I beg . . . uh, what do you mean?"

The old woman gave her a hard look. "I mean what I said. You, my girl, have lived a pampered life and have not tasted your share of bitter berries, but you will. You will."

Ruby hated the mean expression on Grandma's face, so she changed the subject.

"Do you want to hear about Mrs. Thornton Elkins tonight? She was raised to be a lady, but now she has no money."

Her grandma said nothing. She would never admit that she enjoyed Ruby's stories.

Ruby spent the next forty minutes talking about Mrs. Thornton Elkins. Then she went to her room and read from her mother's notes before going to bed.

Dear Daddy, A man came to school and taught us acrobatics. He says I am double-jointed. He played French harp. Love, Jo

Dear Daddy, I have a boyfriend. He is fifteen like me. His name is Clay, and you would like him. He is going to help me with algebra. Love, Jo

Dear Daddy, The loneliest sound in the world is the train whistle in the valley at night. Why does Mama hate me? Love, Jo

This last message was in Ruby's head when she woke up in the dead of night to the sound of that train whistle. It was very faint and faraway, and it put an ache in her heart. She wondered if it was the same train that came screaming into Way Down at dawn.

What had her mother thought about when she woke up in this very bed and heard that sad echo in the hills?

Poor Jo as a child had had no choice but to put up with this cranky woman. She had never known Miss Arbutus and Way Down. This forlorn mountain home had been her whole life!

So it was that Ruby grieved at last for her parents. She turned her face into the pillow and cried for the girl who had tried to bring some joy into her lonely existence by hanging wallpaper samples in her room and writing notes on them to her dead father. And she cried for the boy who had grown up without a family, and then had died before he could enjoy a life with his wife and child.

The next evening, Cedar walked into the common room of The Roost to find Miss Arbutus and Lucy Elkins sitting together on a sofa, with Rita between them. They were looking through an album of photos, mostly of Ruby.

"Oh, hello, Cedar!" Lucy Elkins said to him. "I guess you have come to take Rita home?"

He simply nodded and held out a hand for his sister.

This time the little girl was dressed in a canary yellow sundress with daisies on the pockets and around the neckline. It was another of Ruby's hand-me-downs. Rita had dribbled soup beans down the front while eating dinner with Miss Arbutus and her guests.

She offered her cheek to Miss Arbutus and Lucy Elkins for a goodbye kiss. While they were making over her, the door opened again, and three identical girls entered. They were all dressed in white, with blue ribbons in their hair, which this night fell in blond curls around their shoulders.

At the sight of them, Cedar's mouth fell open, and he forgot where he was or who he was.

"Good evening," Lucy Elkins said cheerfully to the girls. Then, to Cedar and Rita, "These are the Fuller triplets. They are . . ."

"I'm Connie Lynn."

"I'm Sunny Gaye."

"And I'm Bonnie Clare."

"Y'all look like a picture," Lucy complimented them. "Don't they, Miss Arbutus?"

Miss Arbutus smiled and nodded.

The girls all spoke at the same time.

"We come to tell you about the prayer meeting."

"It's to be at seven p.m. tomorrow night."

"Across the road at the football field."

And in unison, "We'll be prayin' for Ruby June."

"Thank you," Miss Arbutus said.

Cedar continued staring at the girls, obviously mes-
merized.

"So we'll be seeing you there."

"Don't forget."

"Bring somebody."

"I'll be there," said Lucy Elkins.

"Me too!" Cedar blurted out. "I love prayin' better'n
anything."

The girls turned to him.

"We've heard about your bad mouth."

"Come with a civil tongue in your head."

"Don't dishonor God with your cussin'."

Cedar turned beet red.

"I-I—" he stuttered. "I—" and could not say more.

"Just don't cuss!" Lucy Elkins relieved him of further
effort. "That's all they're asking."

Cedar grabbed Rita's hand and stumbled out the door.
All the way home, he was silently cussing himself out.
They found Robber Bob sitting alone in the rocker on the
front porch.

"Peter's got comic books in his bedroom," Robber Bob
said. "He got 'em free from Mr. Rife at the five-and-dime
store."

Rita hurried inside to join her brothers, but Cedar
perched on a stool beside his father. They sat in silence
for a time.

"Something on your mind, son?" Robber Bob said to
Cedar after a while.

Cedar changed positions on his stool and hooked his feet on the rungs, but didn't say anything.

"It's a nice night," Robber Bob said softly. "I always think of your mama on nights like this."

The lightning bugs were beginning to come out. The evening was still, and they could hear strains of music coming from somebody's radio down the street.

Cedar pulled something white from his pocket and buried his face in it. Robber Bob recognized the item as a lace handkerchief, which he had given to his wife on her birthday.

"It still holds her special smell, don't it?" he said to his son, almost in a whisper.

"Yeah. It smells like vanilla flavoring."

Robber Bob chuckled. "She baked so much for you young'uns, she always smelled like something good to eat."

"Daddy, sometimes I miss her so much I feel like something's bustin' loose in my chest."

"That's your heart breaking, son," his daddy empathized. "I know the feeling."

"Why did she have to die?"

"I don't have the answer to that."

"Sometimes I'm so mad . . . so mad . . ." Cedar could not go on.

"I know, son."

"Tell me about our last Thanksgiving together, Daddy. Remember it for me."

"Well, it was cold," Robber Bob began softly. "I remember she sat there at the hearth with the firelight dancing in her eyes."

Cedar interrupted, "And she was wearing a blue kinda gown thing, and she said she would be on her way by Christmas, didn't she?"

"That's right," Robber Bob said. "She knew she was dying."

"And she told us not to cry. Didn't she, Daddy? Did she really say that, or did I make it up?"

"Yeah, she said it, but she meant not to cry *forever*, Cedar. It's okay to grieve. She would tell you that."

"And she told us that only her body would be dead, that her soul would go on living."

"That's right, Cedar."

"Then where is she?"

"I don't know."

"She said her soul would come back in another body."

"That's what she believed, my boy."

"Do you believe it?"

"I just don't know."

The tears had begun to fall from Cedar's eyes, and he did not try to stop them. "I don't mean to cuss so bad, Daddy. I know it shames you, but sometimes I . . ."

Robber Bob reached out and placed a hand on Cedar's shoulder. "I know, Cedar. You're a good boy at heart. Your mama always did say so."

"But now she would be so ashamed of me!" Cedar sobbed out loud.

Robber Bob took the trembling boy into his arms then, and allowed him to cry against his shoulder.

The very next morning Cedar walked straight into the doctor's office and settled into a chair without ceremony.

"Mr. Doctor, I done it."

"Done what?" Mr. Doctor replied absentmindedly. He was reading a medical journal. He looked up. "Oh, hello, Cedar. What did you do, my boy?"

"You know, I talked to my daddy, and I . . . I bawled like a little bitty baby."

"That's very good," Mr. Doctor said, and smiled. "How do you feel?"

"Lighter."

"It's a beginning."

"What do you mean?"

"I mean bad habits don't go away overnight. We have to work on them."

"You told me there were four steps to take."

"That's right."

"Well, I've took the first three, now what's the fourth one?"

"You have to go to Mrs. Bevins and tell her how sorry you are that you made fun of her."

"Oh."

"Are you willing to do that?"

"I reckon so, but you'll have to admit, Mr. Doctor, she really did look like a bumblebee."

"Mrs. Bevins grew up very poor, Cedar. She loved pretty clothes, but she had to wear feed-sack dresses and hand-me-downs from her sisters. It was painful to her, and she promised herself that when she grew up, she would have nice things and always try to look attractive.

"When she married Mr. Bevins, who is a generous man, he indulged her little vanities. And they have a very happy marriage because of it."

"I still say she looked like a bumblebee," Cedar mumbled stubbornly.

"That may be, but your opinion doesn't count, nor does mine. Mrs. Bevins believes her taste in clothes is impeccable, and in the long run, it's only what one thinks of oneself that matters."

28

I NEED TO USE THE PHONE, LUCY."

It was a sticky day in August, and Miss Arbutus had come out of her room after taking a nap. She had not slept well the night before.

Surprised, Lucy Elkins dropped the black phone into its cradle, and Miss Arbutus picked it up.

"Do you know the sheriff's number, Lucy?"

"Yes, it's Olive-2002," Lucy said, and she dialed the number for Miss Arbutus.

"Sheriff," Miss Arbutus said after a moment, "this is Arbutus Ward. I have something very important to tell Detective Holland. Can you get him over here?"

Pause.

"That's right, it's about the night Ruby Jo came to us. Call me when he arrives, and I will come to your office."

Another pause.

"So you will both come over here, then? Fine. Let me know when. I'll meet you in the common room."

Later on in the afternoon, Lucy Elkins answered when the sheriff called back.

"Tell Miss Arbutus that Detective Holland is on his way, and we will come to The Roost together after supper."

Of course, several people just happened to pick up the phone and overhear both these conversations, and before long every person in Way Down knew that Miss Arbutus had used the telephone to talk to the sheriff. Furthermore, she had told him that she had something important to say about Ruby, and she would say it to the sheriff and the detective in the common room of The Roost after supper.

As Miss Arbutus and Lucy Elkins finished clearing the supper dishes, the townspeople began to arrive. They came in twos and threes. They did not say why they were there, and nobody asked. Mr. Gentry and Miss Worly welcomed them. Miss Arbutus had disappeared into her room to prepare herself mentally.

The people greeted one another and chatted in low tones as if they were in church. They talked about the weather and the price of sugar, about recipes and the health of their families, anything but Ruby and what Miss Arbutus might have to say to the detective.

As Sheriff Reynolds and Detective Holland approached The Roost, the detective turned to the sheriff and said, "What's all this? Why are these people here?"

"Oh, they're just curious," the sheriff said. "They want to hear what Miss Arbutus has to say."

"But Miss Arbutus may feel that her privacy is being invaded."

"Not at all," the sheriff responded. "If Miss Arbutus had wanted to keep this private, she would not have used the telephone."

Inside the common room, the two men found that comfortable chairs had been reserved for them. They sat down and faced the most comfortable chair of all, which was also vacant, obviously being reserved for Miss Arbutus.

No sooner were the lawmen settled than Miss Arbutus came out of her room and walked down the short hallway and into the common room. All was quiet as she entered, elegantly dressed in an ashes-of-roses silk dress. Her hair was tastefully done in a high French twist, and small patches of color could be detected on her cheekbones and on her lips.

A murmur of approval rose from the group. She smiled a bit nervously at the people and went directly to her chair.

The Reeders were seated on cushions on the hearth, and at sight of Miss Arbutus, little Rita tried to pull away from her father, but he would not let her go. The people made brief friendly comments such as "Good evening, Miss Arbutus," "How nice you look tonight, Miss Arbutus," "What a lovely dress!"

There were also remarks about the appearance of The Roost: how comfortable it was, how pleasant, how nicely the ceiling fans cooled the room, even with all the people in it.

Those who could not squeeze into the common room stayed on the porch. Some of them crowded around the open windows, hoping to hear better. When Miss Arbutus spoke to the detective, all other voices fell silent.

"Thank you for coming this long distance, Detective Holland. As I told the sheriff, I do have something important to tell you, and I don't want to waste your time, so I will begin."

She cleared her throat and looked at her hands, apparently searching for just the right words. In the lull, the soft hum of the fans could be heard.

"I will begin in March of 1944," Miss Arbutus said at last. "As many of you may remember, my dear father, Lucas Ward, passed away that month. He was the last member of my family, and I had spent the previous ten years of my life taking care of him. We were very close, and I was more grief-stricken than I can say. I had no family, no husband or children who needed me. I was the last Ward left in Way Down, and I could hardly bear the emptiness. So I fell into a deep depression.

"In fact, I found it difficult to get out of bed in the mornings. I felt I no longer had a purpose in life. That was the state I found myself in as summer approached. I knew that I could not go on in this way. I wanted to die."

Sympathetic sounds could be heard in the room.

"From the time I was very young, I have had vivid dreams, and in this time of trouble, they were even more so. For three nights in a row I heard a young child crying for its mother. It was a very troubling, touching cry, and in my dreams, I searched and searched, but to no avail.

"Finally, on the fourth night, as I drifted into dreams, I slipped way down deep inside myself for answers. And there I found the other me. Let me explain: I have learned that inside each of us are two beings. One is the conscious self, the one we present to the world. And the other is the wiser self, the one who slumbers in the heart with the wisdom of the ages.

"That night the wise one told me that a treasure lay waiting for me. And she would show me where it was. I mistakenly supposed that she was going to take me to the legendary treasure of Way Down, and I was thrilled. But suddenly I found myself in a strange place away from here.

"I was on the top of a mountain right under the stars. Before me was a weather-beaten house with a large porch, and on the porch were seven children sleeping in the moonlight. But I had eyes only for the smallest one. I knew I had found my treasure.

"She lay on one side with her thumb in her mouth. She had cried herself to sleep, and she took short, quick breaths—you know what I mean? She had the snubs. That's what I've heard mothers call it."

Miss Arbutus looked toward Mr. Doctor. "I think it's something like hyperventilation, isn't it, Mr. Doctor?"

Mr. Doctor nodded. "Yes, it happens when children cry so long and hard, they can't get a good breath."

Miss Arbutus continued. "Well, that's what it was. Tears still glistened on the toddler's cheek. The fine bright hair stuck to her neck and forehead in tiny curls, for it was a warm night.

" 'Your treasure,' the wise one said to me. 'Her mother and father have died. She is bullied and teased by the other children here. And she's just an aggravation to the adults. Take her home, for she will be stifled here and unloved, her gentle spirit broken.'

"I asked no questions. I bunched up my white nightgown and got down on my hands and knees beside the child. I touched her cheek and spoke softly to her. 'Come with me.'

"When she woke up and saw me, a great, wonderful smile lit up her face. She said, 'Mommie!' and hugged my neck.

"I said to her, 'Let's ride horsie!' And I scrunched down right beside her so that she could crawl onto my back.

"When she climbed up she was giggling. 'Wide hossie! Hossie!' she said.

"On all fours I leapt around in the yard for a few minutes to please her. Then I rose up with the little thing clinging to my neck. I clutched her chubby legs around my waist, and set off for home."

29

AT THAT VERY MOMENT ON YONDER MOUNTAIN, GOLDIE Combs and Ruby stood facing each other in the kitchen.

"You sneaked up there and took that picture without permission!" Goldie Combs yelled.

"They are my parents," Ruby said. "I felt the picture was mine."

"You stole it," her grandma said.

Ruby had lost so much weight and sleep that she did not look like the same girl who had once thrived at The Roost. She looked more like a waif who had no one to care for her.

While Ruby had been out picking flowers after supper, Grandma had gone into her room. She had seen the picture tacked on the wall and confronted Ruby when she came back in.

In the previous days Grandma had become more and more difficult. Nothing, not even Ruby's stories of Way Down, could keep her in a good mood.

Ruby still clutched the flowers in her hand. "Please, Grandma, I would like to have the picture back."

Though she remained polite, she was beginning to tremble. She had never felt such a terrible emotion as this. It was almost as if . . . as if she would like to scream at her grandma . . . or worse yet, hit her!

"You had it stored away in an attic where you never looked at it." Ruby tried to reason with the woman.

"If there's one thing I hate, it's a thief!" Grandma said nastily.

Ruby carefully placed the flowers in the sink, then went to her room and sat down on the bed. She closed her eyes and began to count her breaths. It was a trick she had learned from Miss Arbutus. Presently she felt all her anger drain away, and peace settled over her.

She walked back into the kitchen and found Grandma just as she had left her. Her eyes narrowed as Ruby approached.

"Grandma, it's time for me to go home."

"You *are* home!" Grandma snapped.

Ruby reached out and placed a hand on Goldie Combs's arm. "No, Grandma, this is not my true home."

But Grandma shrugged her away. "I am your legal guardian. You can't leave me."

"I have to. I'm suffocating here."

Then Ruby walked into her room again, pulled her suitcase from under the bed, and began to pack her things.

Goldie Combs walked to her doorway. "You mean *now*?" she shrieked at Ruby. "You are leaving right *now*?"

"Yes, I'm going to walk down to Uncle Chris's house and ask him to drive me to Way Down. If he won't do it, then I'll call Miss Arbutus, and she will send somebody for me."

"But it's nearly dark. It'll be pitch-black before you get to Chris's house!"

"I'm not afraid."

"You can't do this to me again, Jolene!"

"I'm not Jolene, Grandma. I'm Ruby Jo, and I have to go. The judge said I should come back to see him after my visit, and now my visit is over."

"We'll just see about that!"

"I'm sorry for you," Ruby went on in the same calm voice. "I want to help you, but I can't stay here without . . ." Ruby searched for the right words. "I don't know exactly know how to explain it, Grandma, but I feel like . . . if I stayed here, something in me would . . . shrivel up and die."

Goldie Combs studied the face of the girl for a long time before she said, "You sound just like your mama."

With that, it seemed Grandma had run out of steam. She suddenly looked older, sicker, as she walked slowly back to her bedroom.

A few minutes later, from the front door, Ruby called, "Goodbye, Grandma. I have to hurry now."

"Just wait until morning," Grandma said, but Ruby did not hear her.

She closed the door behind her and hurried along the path, eager to be at the bottom of the mountain before total darkness fell upon her. Already the woods seemed murky, as in her dreams.

Could she really do this? Could she find her way in the dark? Might she wander off the path and into those scary trees? She looked back at the house once, then clutched the suitcase tightly, and plunged into the woods.

30

THERE WAS SUCH A HUSH IN THE COMMON ROOM, MISS Arbutus had to glance around at the faces to make sure they were not asleep. Quite the contrary, the people were hanging on to every word she uttered. Eyes were wide and mouths were gaping.

Rita Reeder had managed to get away from Robber Bob and moved toward Miss Arbutus. She smiled at the child and lifted her gently onto her lap.

"I skimmed over the earth like the wind." Miss Arbutus continued her story. "My feet barely touched the ground. I often travel this way in dreams. I did not know where I was, but I followed my heart down the mountain.

"I soon discovered my hair was blowing into the little girl's face. So I stopped in the woods, and by the light of the moon I found a fine young vine, with which I secured my hair. Then I took the child on my back again, but before I could move on, I saw something—a panther!"

A gasp went around the room.

"He was coming toward us through the woods, his

sleek black body moving as a shark moves through water. The child saw him, too. I could feel her fast puffs of breath against my neck.

"But I assured her this elegant cat would not hurt us. He felt a kinship to me, for he was the last of his kind, and an aching loneliness hung about him like a tangible thing.

"He did run with us, however, but only because he was in awe of me for the speed with which I could travel. He kept up with me for some distance. I could see his green eyes glowing at my heels.

"When I finally leapt ahead and outran him, he let forth that human scream which was heard and feared by the people on the mountain that night. I imagined them cowering in their beds as they watched their moonlit windows."

At this point Rita was playing with Miss Arbutus's hair, gently removing the pins until it fell thick and dark against the rose silk of her dress. A glow of soft lamplight lay about the woman in the chair. With wonder in their eyes, the townspeople looked at her and thought her beautiful.

"Where was she," the men asked themselves, "when I was looking for a wife? Why did I not see her?"

Others were thinking, "Was it her silence that made us think of her as dull?"

Miss Arbutus was caught up in her story and unaware of her transformation in the eyes of the townspeople. She continued.

"With the toddler giggling and whispering 'Hossie! Hossie!' I galloped through the valleys and woods, up and down the mountains, and over the streams.

"At one place I followed the road. Black snakes had come out to sleep on the pavement, for it was still warm from the previous day. But I hopscotched over them, and the little girl giggled.

"In a dark, cool hollow I stopped to rest. The child climbed off my back and played in the creek. Her tears had dried, and I never knew her to cry for her mommie again.

"Then I heard singing. The girl heard it, too, for she was as quiet as the stars. My mother used to tell me that at certain times if you listen, you can hear the hills singing, and I knew that's what it was.

"These hills hold the memories of people who have lived here for more than a thousand seasons, and they sing of lost love, broken hearts, death, but also of rebirth, renewal, second chances. And about children being rescued in dreams."

A sigh went about the room.

"Then we continued our journey into Way Down. It was barely daylight when we perched on the bench in front of the courthouse before going home. I was telling the little one about the people in the town and how much she was going to like them, when suddenly there was a terrific crash, and I woke up with a cry, in my own bed!

"It so happened that the milkman was running late that morning, and in his haste he had dropped a quart of milk on the walkway directly beneath my window. Crash! And I had been startled from sleep.

"In a panic I jumped out of bed and ran about my room, recalling the child. Where was she? Where was she? All I knew was that she was not with me any longer, and my heart broke in two. Should I run down to the courthouse just to see, you know . . . to see?"

It appeared that Miss Arbutus might start weeping with that sad memory of waking up alone.

" 'No!' I told myself. 'It's no use. It's hopeless. It was only a dream. Only a dream. There was no little girl, no treasure.' I don't mind saying the disappointment was almost more than I could bear.

"I moved into the bitter morning like a sleepwalker, asking myself, 'What now? What now?'

"But soon, as you all know, everybody in town was talking about the redheaded toddler found in front of the courthouse. And my heart went soaring again. I did not question how it had happened. It didn't matter. It was true! It was true! My treasure was real!

"When I saw her in the doctor's office that day, she held out her arms for me and cried, 'Hossie! Hossie!' " Miss Arbutus chuckled. "But nobody seemed to notice, and the rest is history.

"Many nights I have gone into her room, just to watch her sleep and to wonder at the magic that brought her into my life. She has told me that a lady comes into her room at night, and she believes it to be her mother. I tell her, 'Yes, I am sure it is your mother.' "

Miss Arbutus sat there with a dreamy expression on her face, apparently finished with her tale.

"What if . . ." Robber Bob spoke up. "What if the milkman had dropped that bottle and you had woke up while you were far away . . . in that holler maybe, or racing with the panther?"

"That's right!" Mr. Shortt chimed in. "Then Ruby June woulda been left out in the woods by herself in the night."

"I have considered that possibility myself," Miss Arbutus said. "The only answer I can find is that the heart has a wisdom of its own."

For a long time there was silence in the room. The people looked at each other, then back at Miss Arbutus.

"I understand . . ." came a whisper from close by. It was Mrs. Bevins. "I understand why you never told anybody before, but why are you telling us now, Miss Arbutus?"

"I wanted you to understand that she was meant to be with me. Y'all can see that, can't you?"

The response was unanimous.

"Definitely."

"Certainly."

"Absolutely."

"If Judge Deel were here this week, I would ask him for help. But even without his advice, I can see the necessity of taking Ruby's case before the Virginia judge again. And when I'm in court, I will have to swear to tell the whole truth."

"We'll stand by you, Miss Arbutus."

"We'll vouch for your character."

"And the way you've brought the girl up to be so fine."

Miss Arbutus was touched.

Again, nobody spoke for a long time. The people could not get enough of staring at Arbutus Ward, whom they felt they were seeing for the first time. Rita continued to play with the long, dark hair. The woman and child smiled tenderly at each other, as if communicating secretly.

Presently soft weeping could be heard, and all eyes went to Mr. Crawford. Somebody handed him a handkerchief, and he mumbled, "I'm sorry, it's just that I see now."

"See what?" Mr. Morgan asked.

"That your true mother is the one who loves you and cares for you."

The people mumbled in agreement.

"I understand something, too." Mr. Farmer spoke up. "I have been drowning in my memories . . . of the war."

Mrs. Farmer reached out and took her husband's hand in hers.

"But now I see how lucky I am to be here . . . now."

Detective Holland looked around the room at the expressions on the people's faces. He did not ask a single question. And he never would.

31

R<small>UBY</small> J<small>O</small>! R<small>UBY</small> J<small>O</small>!"
Ruby stopped dead in her tracks and turned
slowly. She was startled at the sight of a woman in a white
nightgown moving through the woods, calling for her, and
a vague memory passed through her mind.

*Miss Arbutus in her long white nightgown in these woods.
She and Miss Arbutus running in the moonlight!*

But no . . . it was not Miss Arbutus. It was Grandma.
Ruby set the suitcase down and waited.

Grandma waved something in one hand. "Ruby Jo!
I've brought the picture for you. You can have it back!"

Ruby was too surprised to respond. Goldie Combs approached and handed the photo to her.

"Jo . . . lene," Grandma gasped, slipping back into her
old habit.

"I am not Jolene. I am Ruby," Ruby said with resolve.
"My mother gave me that name because it was her favorite."

Grandma was struggling to breathe.

"Here, sit on my suitcase and rest," Ruby said.

Grandma sat down, picked up the tail of her night-gown, and wiped her face with it.

"How do you know . . ." she managed to say, then paused to suck in air, "about her favorite name?"

"It was one of the first things I read on the wall," Ruby explained.

"That's why I went into your room today," Grandma said. "To see if I could read some of it."

"And could you?"

"I can't read!" Grandma cried out, as if she were in pain.

Ruby was alarmed at the anguish in her grandma's voice. "You mean . . . do you mean the glasses don't help?"

"*No!* The glasses work, but I never learned to read or cipher properly. My mother kept me out of school."

Ruby was speechless. Grandma could not read? She did not know anybody over six who could not read. It was like saying you couldn't breathe or eat or drink water.

"Oh, I can make out some words . . . but . . . I was only a girl, you see. Girls were not important back then. They didn't get much learning."

Grandma seemed like a whipped thing, too beaten to fight anymore. They were quiet for a long time. Finally Grandma's breathing came evenly.

"Come on, I'll walk you home," Ruby said gently as she grasped the woman's elbow.

The two of them hiked back up the path through the woods.

"Ruby was the name she gave that calf one time," Grandma said. "She loved that calf."

"I like my name," Ruby said.

"I can call you Ruby Jo, if that's what you want."

"Yes, it is."

The woods were very dark by then, but Ruby could see the sky ahead where it stretched out wide and deeply turquoise over the top of the mountain.

"And you'll not leave?" Grandma said.

"I can wait until morning."

But Grandma was full of surprises this night. "I want to go with you," she said.

"What?"

"Yes, I've thought and thought about it, ever since you started telling me about Way Down and The Roost and all the people living there. It makes me want to be a better person."

"You want to live at The Roost?"

"Yes, I've never wanted anything so bad. I didn't know there was such a place."

"But, Grandma, it costs money to live there. Miss Arbutus can't afford another charity tenant."

"You said it was two dollars and fifty cents a day!" Grandma said brightly, hopefully. "I can afford that. Chris pays me every week, partly in groceries and partly in cash. I helped him buy the store. If I was eating at The Roost, he would have to give me all cash. And another thing—your grandpa worked for the railroad. So I am able to draw his pension, and Social Security, too, thanks to Franklin D. Roosevelt!"

Ruby's mind went flying. Sure, Grandma probably had more than enough. It was indeed one solution. It was a way in which she could go back and live with Miss Arbutus without a court battle.

"Actually, the permanent residents get a break," Ruby conceded. "They pay only two dollars a day."

"There! See! I can afford that easy."

But Grandma at The Roost? Would it work?

"The Roost is not a nursing home," Ruby said.

"I know."

"Nobody is going to serve your meals in bed."

"I know that! I want to take my meals around that big oak table with the other people. I can picture it in my head." Then after a brief hesitation, she added, "I'm not sick, Jolene . . . I mean Ruby Jo."

"You're not sick?"

"No, I'm just mad. I've been mad for so long, I've nearabout forgot how to be not mad."

"Well, it's not very nice pretending to be sick, and having people wait on you!" Ruby snapped.

"No, it's not!" her grandma agreed. "I ain't been nice."

They stepped up on the porch, where the front door was standing wide open. They went inside and Grandma sat down heavily in a kitchen chair.

"I was born to pretty decent folks over on Bull Mountain," she said. "But my daddy died when I was ten. That was the first time my heart broke in two. Then Mama died, when I was still a teenager.

"When I was old enough to court, the boy I loved married somebody else, and I had to settle for your grandpa. He brought me over here to live. So I just traded one mountaintop for another. And working for the railroad, he was gone most all the time. Seems like I was isolated from people my whole life.

"When I was just getting to like my husband, he died, too. Then Chris married Max and left me. Next Jolene run away and got married, and I was all alone on this mountain, with no way of ever getting off.

"Yeah, I was mad at the world. I had spent my whole life taking care of my family, cooking for them, waiting on them, cleaning up their messes. And what happens? I'm left all alone.

"When they were having money troubles, Chris brought his wife and six children here to live with me, and I was glad to have them. But you know what they did then? They both got jobs down in the valley. They went off to work every day and I was stuck with taking care of their kids. Then Jolene died and you came to me. I never did appreciate you 'cause you were just one more person to take care of. So when you disappeared, I felt awful guilty.

"When Chris and Max took their kids and moved out, I didn't think I could take the loneliness. I wanted to hit somebody, hurt somebody. Instead I played sick so Chris would have to come back and take care of me like I had took care of everybody all my life. I didn't count on him sending strangers to tend my needs. So I got madder and madder and meaner and meaner.

"But now, Ruby Jo, having you here with me, it's been like having Jolene with me again. And I realized how much I loved her, and missed her. I want to be with you, Ruby Jo—I want to spend time with my granddaughter. I wouldn't have to be mad or mean no more. I might even be happy in a place like Way Down."

"And what if you're not happy?" Ruby said rather harshly. "Are you going to be bigmouthed and bossy, and embarrass me in front of my friends?"

Her grandma looked at her with weary eyes, but said nothing.

"At The Roost we all get along," Ruby went on. "We respect each other, and we don't have people yelling and hollering and ordering other people around. Nobody wants to live with a bully!".

"I know, I know," her grandma answered rather meekly. "All I can say is, I'll try to get along. I want to be there with you, Ruby Jo. And I want to meet those people and live in that town. I want to sit on the porch and watch people go by. I want to talk to somebody different every day, and have friends for the first time in my life. Maybe somebody will teach me to read."

Ruby immediately thought of Miss Worly. Wouldn't she love that challenge? But still Ruby felt a nagging doubt. Sure, somebody could teach Grandma to read, but could you teach a woman her age to change her mean-tempered ways?

"Come in here," Ruby said, pointing to her room, "and let me read you what your daughter—my mama—had to say."

Slowly, heavily, her grandma got up from her chair and followed Ruby into her room. Ruby began reading aloud among the parasols. She read for a long time without glancing up.

"Why does Mama hate me?" were the last words from Ruby's lips before she turned and faced her grandma. "Now aren't you ashamed . . ."

But she didn't go on. Grandma was crying.

All of the bad temper was forgotten as Ruby suddenly felt a great surge of pity for her grandma. Yes, it was no wonder she was mad at the world. She had lived a very hard and sad life.

"Grandma," she said gently, "I think you'll be welcome at The Roost."

32

THE NEXT MORNING THE ROOST RESIDENTS WERE AWAK-
ened by an unfamiliar racket. It was Mr. Crawford's
typewriter. He appeared for breakfast with a smile on his
face and announced that he was planning to finish his
book by Christmas. After eating, he went back to writing.

When Miss Arbutus emptied the trash later that day,
she found a phonograph record in it. She was surprised to
see it was Mr. Crawford's "Laura." Carefully she dug it
out and put it away. It was a nice song, and somebody
might want to hear it again someday.

That afternoon, as Miss Arbutus and Lucy Elkins
were in the common room having a cup of tea and cookies
together, Rita Reeder walked in with a big smile on her
face. She had come alone, wearing a red sunsuit that Ruby
had worn when she was five.

"Well, look at you!" Lucy Elkins said to the child.
"What a big girl you are to come all by yourself!"

Rita climbed onto Miss Arbutus's lap, picked up a

cookie, and spoke her first words since her mother had died.

"Ruby June is coming home."

When Chris Combs and his three sons arrived at the house on Yonder Mountain with groceries the following Saturday, they were surprised to see Ruby and Goldie Combs sitting on the front porch, chatting and laughing together like old friends.

"Howdy do, boys!" Grandma called out to them pleasantly. "Y'all come on over and set a spell. We've got some talking to do."

Uncle Chris and his sons were so amazed, they didn't think about running away or protesting. They set their grocery sacks down on the edge of the porch and simply stared at Grandma Combs.

"I'm moving on," the woman said. "Going to live in town at The Roost. Ruby is leaving today, and she'll need a ride to Way Down. If you can't take her, Chris, then she'll call from your place and have Miss Arbutus send somebody for her."

Grandma's face was bright with excitement, but the four male faces were blank, and all eight of their eyes remained wide with wonder.

"That's right," Ruby joined in. "I'll have to speak with Miss Arbutus first, but I'm sure she'll say it's okay."

"As for me, I'm gonna need some help from the three

of you boys," Grandma said. "I have to go through my stuff. It's been building all these years. I'll be packing some of it to take with me, and I'll give the rest away, if anybody wants it.

"I'll pay you to help me pack and carry stuff off this mountain. I'll not bark at you."

The boys looked at their grandma doubtfully.

"I promise," Grandma said.

Then Ruby was finally on her way home. She walked through the woods and down the mountain with Uncle Chris and her cousins. Jeff and Sam turned out to be more likable than Sidney. They did not tease her.

That very afternoon Uncle Chris took her home. She arrived at The Roost as the tenants were assembling in the common room to wait for the supper bell. When Miss Arbutus heard all the commotion from the front room, she knew that Ruby had returned. She and Lucy Elkins took off their aprons and hurried in to greet her.

It was a wonderful meal, all full of bubbling laughter and good food. Ruby had so much to talk about, she could hardly fit her food in between the words.

After dinner Miss Arbutus helped her put her things away, and they talked about Grandma.

"She's not all that bad once you get to know her," Ruby explained. "In fact, y'all will probably get along just fine."

"Of course she must come and live with us!" Miss Arbutus said to Ruby. "It's the answer I've been praying for!"

33

AFTER HER DISCUSSION WITH MISS ARBUTUS ON THE PARticulars of Grandma's coming to Way Down, Ruby went out to see Jethro. The goat was so tickled, he didn't know how to act. He scampered all over the yard and up the woodpile, then back to Ruby for more hugs. He was headed for the woodpile again when two figures came around the side of the house and entered through the gate.

"Peter! Cedar!" Ruby squealed, and almost hugged them both, but managed to control herself.

Peter just stood there grinning. He searched his brain for something to say, but found himself tongue-tied.

Not so with Cedar. "Wanna go hang around town?" he asked Ruby.

"Sure."

So the three of them ventured toward Busy Street to see what they could see on a Saturday night.

As they neared Mrs. Rife's house, they spotted the old

woman sitting on her porch with a small pile of rocks beside her. She held one of them in her hand.

"Uh-oh!" Ruby whispered. "There she is, just waiting for us."

"But I heard she quit throwing rocks!" Peter said.

"Yeah," Cedar joined in. "At least, she's trying to break the habit."

They walked by cautiously with one eye on Mrs. Rife all the way, barely daring to breathe.

Mrs. Rife just sat there holding the rock and mumbling to herself.

"What's she saying?" Ruby whispered.

But at that moment Mrs. Rife spoke up. "I am *not* going to throw this rock!" And louder still, *"You hear me, you mangy strays? I am* not *going to throw this rock!"*

"Watch out!" Ruby hollered, and the three of them broke into a run. The rock sailed by their heads, missing all three. They ran, laughing so hard they could hardly breathe.

At a safe distance they finally stopped. Gasping, they bent over and braced their palms on bent knees to catch their breath again. Only then did they look back. The old woman was sitting again, her eyes peeling the neighborhood for other kids to harass.

"She can't quit," Ruby managed to say. "She's about as addicted to rock-throwing as Mr. Farmer is to liquor."

"Not anymore!" Cedar said. "I met up with him this morning. He was helping Mrs. Farmer deliver the mail, and he told me he hasn't had a drop of liquor in days."

"Good for him!"

"Cedar can tell you how hard it is to break a habit," Peter said. "Right, Cedar?"

"I don't wanna discuss it," Cedar replied.

"He has to do a chore for Mrs. Bevins every time he says a cuss word!" Peter informed Ruby with a wink.

"Talk about something else!" Cedar said hotly.

"Okay." Peter relented, and turned his attention back to Ruby. "How was your visit to Yonder Mountain?"

"Not bad. My grandma is coming here to live at The Roost."

"No kiddin'? When?"

"Next week. She had a lot of things to sort out at her house. My cousins are helping her. Me and Miss Arbutus have to get her room ready for her."

"Where you gonna put her?"

"Well, I guess you heard Mr. Gentry and Miss Wordy are getting married and moving out?"

"Yeah, we heard that."

"So I am going in Miss Wordy's 'spacious pastel boudoir.' Grandma will be next door to me, and we are fixing up my old room for Rita when she comes to spend the night."

"I'm glad y'all are taking such an interest in Rita," Peter said. "Now I won't feel so guilty running off to band practice in the evenings."

"You're going to play in the band?"

"I sure am! Mr. Gentry has been working with me on the drums. He says I have a rare talent for it. One of his drummers is graduating this year, and he wants me to take his place."

As they entered Busy Street, it seemed the whole town had turned out to welcome Ruby home, and her heart swelled.

34

RUBY WOKE UP, AND FOR A FEW SECONDS COULD NOT RE-member where she was. Then her face broke into a smile in the darkness. Yes, she was sleeping in her own bed at The Roost. And nobody would ever take her away again.

After her return from town, she and Miss Arbutus had sat at the dressing table talking for a long time, and Ruby had learned about her magical journey over the mountains and valleys with Miss Arbutus when she was a toddler.

"On Yonder Mountain I learned about my mama and daddy," she told Miss Arbutus. "I wish they hadn't died, but the way I got here . . . why, you know, Miss Arbutus . . . that story tells me for certain that I am supposed to be here with you! And I think it's what they must have wanted for me."

Now it was three in the morning, and something had awakened Ruby. She lay there and listened.

She could hear voices outside and see headlight beams

sweeping across her ceiling. She jumped onto her knees and pulled the pansy curtains aside.

Yes! It was the carnival! They were moving in for Kids' Day, which would be on Monday. She watched the long string of covered trucks and colorful vans that carried the Ferris wheel, the merry-go-round, the Tilt-a-Whirl, and other carnival paraphernalia and people.

Ruby thought of previous Kids' Days in Way Down. First Mayor Chambers always made a short speech in which he told the kids how much they were loved and treasured above and beyond all things. He explained that Kids' Day was just a little token of the town's appreciation. And he always ended by saying that the real treasure of Way Down was its children.

Ruby looked at the hills silhouetted against the night sky and remembered the many nights she had whispered in the darkness, "Woo-bee is right here waiting for you."

Now she could put that thought to rest. No more waiting.

She picked up the picture from her nightstand. In the moonlight she could make out the smiles on those three happy faces. She thought of her mother as a little girl, lonely and unloved on Yonder Mountain. And she thought of her father growing up in an orphanage where he was probably neglected.

"But I will always remember you happy and smiling like this," she whispered to them.

Then she sank back into her bed and closed her eyes. Fanning out like a boat's wake behind her she could see the past—those sweet, dreamy days in Way Down, the laughter and joy, the Christmases and birthdays and last days of school, the people she had known for a night or a season or a lifetime. And yes, there would be many such wonders ahead!

But this would probably be her last Kids' Day. Now that she had a real birthday, she knew she would be thirteen on October 2, and too old for such stuff. She would grow up and suffer through algebra and acne, high heels and lost loves, and other bitter berries.

But for the time being, she was still only twelve, and she would savor every moment. For *now* there was the upcoming carnival and Kids' Day and a full moon shining way down deep between the mountains of West Virginia.

DISCUSSION QUESTIONS

1. Describe the town of Way Down Deep. Compare and contrast it with your own neighborhood or town.

2. How did the townspeople react when Bob Reeder tried to rob the bank? Would you have responded the same way? Explain.

3. Peter Reeder says, "Mama used to say that nobody comes into our lives by accident. We have something to learn from everybody we meet." Do you agree with this statement? Why or why not?

4. Why does Cedar Reeder have cussitis? How would you define cussitis? How is it cured?

5. Ruby learns about her parents from reading her mama's writing on the wallpaper at her grandmother's house. What does she learn about her mother and father? About her grandmother?

6. Describe Miss Arbutus and her relationship with Ruby. What do the townspeople think of Miss Arbutus? Do their opinions change when she tells the story of how Ruby arrived in Way Down Deep? If so, how do they change?

7. How does Grandma Combs change from the time Ruby arrives at Grandma's house to her move to The Roost? What were the reasons for this change?

8. Who is your favorite resident of Way Down Deep? Describe the character and explain why you like him or her.

9. Were you surprised that Miss Arbutus allowed Grandma Combs to move to The Roost? Do you think this will change Ruby's relationship with Miss Arbutus?

10. *Way Down Deep* is a story about family, friends, the love that binds people together, and what it takes to make a place truly home. What do you learn about family from reading this story? How do you define home?

RUTH WHITE

William Anderson

What did you want to be when you grew up?
I wanted to be a movie star, of course. Didn't everybody?

When did you realize you wanted to be a writer?
I always wanted to be a writer as well as a movie star. I made up stories and wrote them down as soon as I was able to write.

What's your most embarrassing childhood memory?
In second grade, I was busted for cheating on a spelling test. I was so ashamed, I never cheated again.

What's your favorite childhood memory?
On cold winter nights, curling up with my mother and sisters, all in one bed, while Mom read to us.

As a young person, who did you look up to most?
Teachers and preachers because they were educated

What was your favorite thing about school?
Recess and lunch. I was never a great student, but I did like reading.

What was your least favorite thing about school?
Arithmetic. I still don't get numbers.

What were your hobbies as a kid? What are your hobbies now?
I collected movie-star magazines and comic books. Today, I collect movies on DVD and audiobooks. So I haven't changed that much.

What was your first job, and what was your "worst" job?
My first job was babysitting. It paid fifty cents an hour. My worst job was working in the cafeteria in college.

How did you celebrate publishing your first book?
I went out to dinner with my family. I also bought myself a gold chain necklace that I still wear often.

Where do you write your books?
I used to write with a pen and paper while I sat in the middle of my bed. Today, I have an office with a computer in my home. It's easier, but it was more fun the other way.

What sparked your imagination for *Way Down Deep*?
I read a newspaper article about a child who was abandoned in a small Midwestern town, apparently by someone who was just passing through. Unfortunately, that child died of exposure, and the incident stayed on my mind for a long time. I finally decided to give that child a life in a loving environment, and the result was *Way Down Deep*.

Of the books you've written, which is your favorite?
Weeping Willow is my favorite because it is more true to life than any of my other books. It was a work of love.

What challenges do you face in the writing process, and how do you overcome them?
Distractions. Like other writers, I will find excuses not to get down to work. Getting started is the most difficult part. Once you get into it, the story comes alive for you again, and the writing flows. I find if I can make myself write just one sentence, then just one more, I am on my way.

Which of your characters is most like you?
Tiny Lambert in *Weeping Willow*, also Ginny Shortt in *Sweet Creek Holler*

What makes you laugh out loud?
When I was a kid, it was Abbot and Costello and The Three Stooges. Today, it's *America's Funniest Home Videos.*

What do you do on a rainy day?
About the same as any other day, except that I don't walk. I exercise indoors.

What's your idea of fun?
Going on a trip with my daughter and grandson. We recently went back to the mountains where I was born and raised. We saw my old high school and stayed in a cabin at the Breaks Interstate Park for three days, hiked, and had a picnic. That was fun.

What's your favorite song?
I have dearly loved so many songs over the years that it's hard to pick a favorite, but I would say my all-time favorite is "Bridge

Over Troubled Water" from the '60s by Simon & Garfunkel. In the last few years, I have loved "After the Gold Rush" by Emmylou Harris, Linda Ronstadt, and Dolly Parton. The harmony is absolutely perfect.

Who is your favorite fictional character?
Probably Mick Kelly in *The Heart Is a Lonely Hunter*

What was your favorite book when you were a kid? Do you have a favorite book now?
As a kid, the Laura Ingalls Wilder series, and now, *To Kill a Mockingbird*

What's your favorite TV show or movie?
I like *American Idol* very much because I love to hear young, talented singers. Some favorite movies are *Blast from the Past*, *Yentl*, and *The Phantom of the Opera*.

If you were stranded on a desert island, who would you want for company?
Other than my daughter and grandson? Perhaps some really funny middle-school kids.

If you could travel anywhere in the world, where would you go and what would you do?
Italy, and I would travel around the countryside, staying at small village inns.

If you could travel in time, where would you go and what would you do?
I would go to the Middle Ages and try to teach people about cleanliness and health. Of course, I would probably be burned as a witch.

What's the best advice you have ever received about writing?

From Anne Lamott's book *Bird by Bird*, I learned not to be afraid of writing really bad first drafts. They are supposed to be bad. The good writing comes with editing those bad first drafts.

Do you ever get writer's block? What do you do to get back on track?

Yes, and once again, I use the one-sentence rule. I make myself write just one sentence. That usually leads me to another sentence, but if it doesn't, I try again the next day—just one sentence.

What do you want readers to remember about your books?

That, regarding place and time, most of them are authentic. These places and some of these characters actually lived.

What would you do if you ever stopped writing?

Die

What do you like best about yourself?

My ability to change. It's a rare gift.

Do you have any strange or funny habits? Did you when you were a kid?

Yes and yes. I did and do make lists of everything, methodically plan my daily activities, my budget, my exercise routine, my diet.

What do you consider to be your greatest accomplishment?

Raising a beautiful, healthy, well-adjusted daughter, who is a good citizen and an asset to society

What do you wish you could do better?
Play the piano

What would your readers be most surprised to learn about you?
That I totally dislike fantasy, vampires, and werewolves

Garnet feels abandoned after her mother leaves her at her Aunt June's house. But her aunt thinks she's there for a reason. Aunt June's on a quest to find God, and as she battles cancer she drags her niece to different religious services every week in an attempt to find Him.

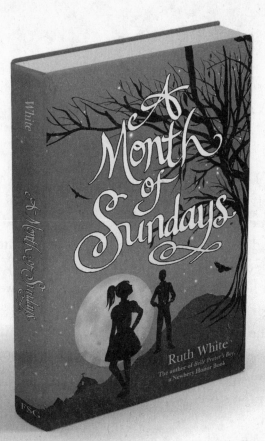

Keep reading for an excerpt of

A Month of Sundays

by Ruth White

I

*B*efore I was born fourteen years ago, my dad, August Rose, left my mom, Betty Rose, for a carnival singer. With no close kin, and nobody to help her in a pinch, Mom had to take some pretty lousy jobs over the years. Of course, living in Elkhorn City, Kentucky, where nobody lives a posh life, her expectations were not that high to start with.

For the last few years Mom has been working in a grocery store. Above the market is a three-room dump where we live with a woman named Lily, who also works in the store. Yes, it gets pretty crowded, and I do resent it.

I have asked Mom maybe a hundred times why she doesn't chase my dad down and wring some money out of him, but she has been too stubborn and proud to do that. So while I've been wearing last year's shoes and dreaming over dresses in the Sears catalog that I'll never have, Mom has clung to her precious pride, like it's worth more than me.

Recently, Mom's childhood friend, Grace Colley, came back to Elkhorn City after a long absence, but immediately began to wish she hadn't. So do I. She and Mom are thick as thieves.

It's the last week of school, and I come home one day to find them at the kitchen table with their heads together, doing some figuring on a piece of paper. And I can tell by their expressions that something is going on.

When Mom looks up and sees me, she says with excitement in her voice, "Garnet, I have finally got enough money saved to get out of here. We're going to Florida!"

"Florida? You mean to live?"

"If I can find work there, yes. They've been talking on the radio about Daytona Beach. It's the hot place for jobs right now."

I sit down at the table. Florida!

"When are we leaving?"

Mom does not answer right away, and her eyes meet Grace's.

"Garnet, honey," Mom says at last. "I was thinking that maybe Grace and I would go first, and find work.

When I've saved enough, I'll send bus fare money, and you can join us down there. It shouldn't take long once I have a job."

All my blood rushes to my face. "So that's what you were thinking, huh? You're going to leave me here with Lily?"

"No, of course not. I've written a letter to your dad's sister, June, asking her if you can stay with her."

"But we don't even know each other!"

"It's time to remedy that situation," Mom says.

"Why can't I go with you?"

"Chiefly because of the expense," Mom says. "Three people on the road costs more than two. We're going on a shoestring as it is."

I can only glare at her because there are certain things you can't say to your mom, no matter how mad you are.

"Besides," Mom goes on, "you would have to stay by yourself a lot while we're looking for work, and I would worry about you in a strange place."

And it's settled. Do I have any say in the matter? Do I ever?

Aunt June answers Mom's letter right away, saying she had absolutely no idea her brother had a child.

"Why on earth would August keep something like that from me?" she says in her letter. "Of course Otis and I would be thrilled to meet April Garnet, and look after her while you are finding work in Florida."

She says she's sorry August will not be there to see me, but she has no idea where that rascal is. He has not been around in more than a year.

The following Sunday we are in Grace's Packard on our way to Black River, Virginia, about two hours from Elkhorn City, where I will live among strangers for an indefinite period of time. I don't speak to Mom all the way there.

"I'm sure this is her house," Mom says when we arrive and find nobody home. "I remember how it hangs out into the road, because it's built on a curve. And how could I ever forget this funny green color?"

I finally have to break my silence. "Didn't you tell her we were coming today?"

"Not exactly," Mom says. "I just told her sometime this weekend."

I do an exaggerated eye roll, then turn my back to her.

"Don't be so grumpy!" Mom says.

We take my suitcase from Grace's car, and the three of us sit down in some chairs on the porch. Grace looks at her watch. It's clear she wants to hightail it out of here as soon as she can. It's a pretty busy road here, and some of the cars slow down to look at us as they pass. Not only that, but there are houses lining both sides of the road, and people are craning their necks to see out the windows. Some of them even come outside. I guess they can't stand not knowing who we are.

Directly across the road is a small brick store that says Richards' Grocery on the window. A man and woman are sitting in rocking chairs out front.

The sun is hiding behind a rising storm cloud. A wind begins to stir the trees on the hills that rise up all around this valley.

"Hey, y'all! Yoo-hoo!"

It's a woman waving at us from the house beside the store.

"Wonder what she wants?" Mom says, and raises her hand to wave back.

"Are you waiting on Otis and June Bill?" the woman calls.

"Yes we are!" Mom replies.

"Well, they went to the cemetery to lay flowers on the graves of their kin."

Right. It's Decoration Day.

"But they should be back here drek'ly," the woman goes on. "Who are y'all anyhow?"

Mom sighs. "I'll go talk to her."

And she leaves the porch to cross the road and speak with the nosy woman. In a few moments Mom comes back.

"That's Mrs. Mays," she says. "And those two in the rocking chairs are Mr. and Mrs. Richards, who own the store. They are just tickled to death to meet August's *wife*." Mom smirks as she emphasizes the word "wife."

Technically, Mom is still Dad's wife since they never got a divorce.

"They will be even more tickled to meet August's little girl whenever she feels like coming over to see them."

"August's little girl?" I say sourly. "I wonder how many times I'll have to hear that?"

Mom and Grace laugh at me. They are in a jolly mood. Well, good for them!

"And I learned June and Otis have two boys," Mom says. "Their names are Emory and Avery."

The rain starts coming down in big sparkling drops, and still we wait for more than an hour. Finally a brand-new '57 Plymouth Fury, nearly the same color as the house, comes rolling up beside the porch. Inside there's a man driving, and a woman on the seat beside him. In the back are two good-sized boys, maybe ten and twelve. Must be the Bills, my long-lost kin.

2

Aunt June is a little bitty woman, no more than five feet tall and about a hundred pounds. Uncle Otis is big and burly with a bushy beard on his face. He looks like a gorilla. The boys are ordinary-looking. Everybody has blue eyes.

"I'll declare! I'll declare!" Aunt June says as she pulls Mom into a hug. "Good to see you again, Betty."

Uncle Otis silently shakes Mom's hand, the boys mumble something, Mom introduces Grace, then they all turn to me.

"And this is your niece, April Garnet Rose," Mom says to Aunt June.

I try to smile at my dad's sister. After all, none of this is her fault.

"August's little girl!" she says, and hugs me. There it

is again. Then she stands back and studies me. "I think you have your daddy's eyes, but you look more like your mom."

Mom and Grace keep edging toward the porch steps. They can't wait to get away.

"Y'all come in and have something to eat and drink," Aunt June says to them. "You don't want to leave in this rain."

"We really need to hit the road," Mom says. "We've got a long drive ahead of us."

Grace nods in agreement and glances at her watch again.

"Well, don't worry about April Garnet. We'll take good care of her."

Mom looks at me, then comes over and puts an arm around me.

"I promise to write, sweetie, as soon as I have an address where you can reach me," she says. "Then we can make arrangements for you to join us." And she kisses me on the cheek. "Now, don't you cry, hear me?"

"I'm not crying," I mumble.

"You look like you're about to."

"Well, I'm not! Go on, get out of here!"

And just like that, Mom and Grace are gone.

"I'll declare, I'll declare," Aunt June mumbles.

I'm guessing it's something she says when she can't think of anything else to say.

"Why did your mama bring you here?" the older boy says rudely.

"Hush, now, Emory," Aunt June says to him. "She's your first cousin."

"I thought Madge was our first cousin," says the small boy—Avery, I guess.

"Madge is your first cousin and so is April," Aunt June says.

"That don't make sense," says Avery. "Somebody has to be second."

"I've always been called Garnet," I inform Aunt June, though I've never known why Mom insists on using my middle name.

"Oh, okay, Garnet. We're glad to have you here, aren't we, Otis?"

She turns to her husband, who hasn't yet spoken a word.

"Oh, yeah, sure," he manages to say. "It's a nice surprise."

Surprise? So he didn't know I was coming? It sounds like the boys didn't know either.

"Let's get in out of the rain," Aunt June says. "Emory, take her suitcase."

"Take her suitcase?" he sputters. "Where to?"

"Go on now," Aunt June coaxes him. "Take her suitcase in the house for her. It won't hurt you to do that."

"I'll carry it myself," I say as I grab the suitcase by the handle. "I don't need help."

We go in the house. It's a very strange place. There are rooms shooting off in all directions. It's a maze—that's what it is. Right in the middle of the maze are wooden stairs. I can't tell what's at the top.

"Avery, show Garnet up to the sunporch," Aunt June says.

I wonder what a sunporch is, but I'll not ask.

"Come on, Garnet," Avery says, and I am glad to see he's a friendly, smiling little thing, not a bit like Emory.

Upstairs there are short hallways running in four directions. We turn down one of them to the left and wind up in a room that looks like it was just glued onto the end of the house. The first thing that hits you is all the yellow—a yellow bedspread on a double bed, a yellow skirt on a vanity table, and one yellow wall. The other three sides of the room are big windows with yellow and white café curtains. Rain is slashing against the glass.

"This is our sunporch," Avery says proudly. "Daddy just made it for Mama the other day."

"The other day?"

"I mean he finished it the other day. He's been building on it for a long time."

"It's nice," I say. I mean it. I love it. I don't think I ever saw a brighter room in my life. And I'll bet when the sun shines in here you could get a tan just lying on the bed.

I put my suitcase down and turn to see myself in a mirror over the vanity table beside the door. My face is pale, my shoulder-length blond hair is messy, and my blue eyes have faint shadows under them.

"You sure are pretty," Avery says to me suddenly, and I am so surprised I am speechless. Now, I really feel like I'm going to cry, but I don't.